BEYOND THE LINES

Book two of the kids Like You series

CLAUDIA WHITSITT

BEYOND THE LINES
Copyright © 2016 Claudia Whitsitt
Published in 2016 in the United States

ISBN: 978-0-9963436-3-3

Cover Design by Littera Designs www.litteradesigns.com
Book Formatting by champagneformats.com
Editor: Jean Jenkins

#friendshipiscolorblind

Beyond the Lines is the much awaited sequel to *Between the Lines*, inspired by kids like you in the hopes that you will do your best each and every day to make the world a kinder place.

What Readers Are Saying:

BEYOND THE LINES, the sequel to BETWEEN THE LINES, reunites us with three 5th graders that have become so real to us they could be pushing us on a swing, playing basketball, or jumping rope with us on the playground. We call them by their nicknames and discuss their dilemmas and decisions as if they were sitting next to us on the carpet in our classroom. They are part of us.

These youngsters have the ability to problem solve and the energy to make a difference without resorting to negativity or violence. They make us see clearly that there are ways to overcome adversity and that even as ten year olds, they can make a difference in the way others see the world around them.

BEYOND THE LINES illustrates the importance of sports in the life of children. Through Crackers' quest to play basketball on the boy's team, we meet boys that don't see the difference in gender in sports, and also those that are much less tolerant. The tension created by this storyline teaches us about healthy competition, and ultimately, that girls can do everything boys can do.

The relationships Crackers, Hattie and Beverly Jo have with their parents show us the need for parental support and involvement during our formative years. And, finally, the compassion they have for each other is the same compassion I witness each and every day as I watch my students form friendships I know will last a lifetime.

Crackers, Hattie and Beverly Jo are from three very different walks of life, but they embrace their differences and celebrate their similarities. They learn a lot about life from each other as they help us understand what it means to be more tolerant and empathetic. They support each other through situations that many 5th graders face, and even some situations that are a bit out of the ordinary. Their friendship reminds us life is easier when you have true friends to share it with.

BEYOND THE LINES is a refreshing story of true friendship. Although the main characters are just ten years old, this story speaks to all readers, especially adults. We can all learn a thing or two from these three spunky adolescents!
~Lori LaBoe, 5th grade teacher, Saline, Michigan

After living through the Detroit Riots of 1967, moving to a new school and making new friends, Hattie thought she had figured out what discrimination looked like. Hattie is the eternal optimist, always looking for and dreaming about making the world a better place. Hattie's two best friends are Beverly Jo, who's smart as a whip, and also the only black child in her class, and Crackers. She's the class clown and the school's best athlete (even among the boys). In this sequel to *Between the Lines,* Hattie and her friends discover that discrimination goes beyond the color of skin. The Dream Girls, Hattie, Beverly and Crackers' club, plan an event to help break long-standing prejudices and help redefine school rules that only seem to put up barriers for success. Hattie also learns about her own prejudices and how powerful forgiveness can be. This story is a beautiful tribute to true friendship. #friendshipiscolorblind
~Katherine Pfieffer, Librarian, Ann Arbor, Michigan

For Jenna
Always an inspiration, always
courageous, always in my heart.

CHAPTER ONE

FOUR MONTHS AGO, I THOUGHT MY LIFE WAS OVER. BUT just look at me now. I've gone from a Catholic school kid to a public school student and from a knock-kneed scaredy-cat to a mostly brave girl. Not only that, but I've made the best friends ever. Beverly Jo is not just the smartest girl I know, but the friendliest, and Crackers, well, she's the life of the party, whether there's a party or not.

Which brings me to our 5th grade holiday break celebration, a sleepover at my house. The aromas wafting down the basement stairs right now awaken me in the best possible way—with a gigantic grin on my face. There's not a better smell in the world than bread frying in a custard of milk, eggs and butter, crackling bacon, and warm maple syrup.

I stretch my arms over my head and untangle my sleeping bag from the cocoon its coiled around my legs, peeking out to see if either of my friends' peepers are blinking yet.

"Crackers," I whisper. "Do you smell that?"

She pops up like a Jack in the Box, her blue eyes as wide as her smile, blonde ringlets a tumble around her cheeks. "Woo-hoo, Hattie! Your mom made us breakfast? She's the best mom ever!"

Crackers. Right, as usual. Mom is awfully nice to make us homemade French toast. She usually reserves special breakfasts for Sunday mornings, after church.

"Beverly, wake up." Crackers jiggles the lump inside Beverly's sleeping bag and starts beating it with her pillow.

Beverly doesn't move. She knows Crackers might never stop annoying her, but she likes to at least try to wait her out. Her tactic works. When Beverly doesn't react, Crackers loses interest and cannon fires out of her sleeping bag. "Let's go eat. Lazy bones can join us when she's done getting her beauty rest."

Beverly's huge brown eyes peek out from the dark hole she's cinched around her face. She's like a turtle poking its head out from a shell. "I'm awake. Just thinking."

"It's too early to think," Crackers says. "Let's get some chow."

Beverly eases her bony limbs out from under her covers and rises on her toes, reaching her fingertips to the ceiling and yawning. "Being here with you guys is like a dream come true. I'm so happy, I don't think I ever need to eat again."

Crackers slaps her on the back and about knocks her flat. Beverly is just a wisp of a girl. "You've lost your mind, Bev Jo." Crackers tugs on Beverly's braids. "Can we trade heads for today? I want to see what it's like to be black."

Crackers. Always predictable. Always outrageous.

We tromp upstairs. Sun spills through the kitchen windows. What a treat—Mom has set the table for company. She's cleaned the entire kitchen, too, because not a fleck of dust disrupts the sunbeams. Orange juice sits in dainty jelly jars to the right of each place setting. Even the napkins are fancy-folded in a V. I watch my friends clamber into their seats and begin to devour the meal. This might be the best day of my life.

The phone rings and Mom answers, her telephone voice reminding me of an actress on TV. She's like a secretary who's been instructed to sound like the most pleasant person on the planet. "Hello, Percha residence."

The sight of her tucking the phone into the crook between her shoulder and cheek so she can wipe her hands on her apron makes my heart swell with pride as I remember a few short months ago when Beverly first visited our house. Mom practically held her breath for the entire visit. She's completely changed her tune. Now, she loves Beverly, even if her skin is a different color than ours.

"Oh!" Mom's mouth breaks into an delighted grin. "That's wonderful. Thank you so much for calling. Yes…she will be thrilled. After Christmas break is perfect. Yes…I'll bring her a bit early so she has time to get settled in her new school."

This is one of those times I wish I wasn't such a fan of Nancy Drew. Learning how to read clues comes in handy most times, but while Mom thinks this is delicious news, my heart sinks to my toes and splinters into a million little pieces. My fork drops onto the plate. I can't eat another bite.

"Who was that?" I try to act casual, in spite of the fact that I might just throw up.

Crackers and Beverly continue to chatter about their tasty breakfast and make plans about who will ride in position "A" on the toboggan. Dad has agreed to take us to Rouge Park for a few hours so we can cruise the best sled run in all of Detroit.

I push in my chair and sneak over next to Mom at the sink,

my eyes pleading with her to tell me this isn't so.

"We'll discuss this later, Hattie. Finish your breakfast. No pity parties while your friends are here."

"But, Mom, I don't want to go to St. Mary's. I'm a Crary student. You have to understand." My hands ball into fists, and I fight to keep my voice at a whisper so Crackers and Beverly don't overhear.

"Not now," Mom hushes me.

I need a place to hide. Somewhere no one will ever find me.

I'm dizzy, and grab the counter to keep the room from spinning, or my knees from buckling. The room goes muddy, even though the sun shimmered through the window just a minute ago.

"Hattie? Are you okay?" I hear Beverly from across the room, but she sounds like she's miles away.

White noise fills the kitchen and my ears begin to ring. My limbs go boneless.

Next thing I know, three pairs of eyes are planted on me— Crackers', Beverly's, and Mom's.

"Why Hattie girl, I believe you fainted. Have you ever passed out before? I got my bell rung one time when I crashed my bike into a boulder, but you didn't knock your head when you fell. Do you feel sick?" Crackers plants her hands on her hips the entire time she speaks, and I have a rambling thought about what a great doctor she'd make, or principal of a school, or even President of the United States, the way she takes matters into her own hands whenever there's a crisis.

Bile rises in my throat and my head throbs, but I'll never admit my symptoms or Mom will send my friends home faster than they scarfed down breakfast. I swallow the vile sourness that is in my throat, and when Mom lays a cool washcloth on my forehead, the fuzziness in my vision begins to clear. "I'm not sure what happened."

"Just lay here for a minute." Beverly rests a hand on my shoulder and winks at me. She must have been paying attention and overheard my mom's telephone conversation. Beverly and I have a connection where words don't matter—we pass our hearts back and forth, or live in the same soul sometimes—Beverly just knows. Maybe ESP is real.

My lungs fill with oxygen at the thought, like I'm breathing fresh air for the first time in a week. Beverly's eyes lock on mine, and while Crackers stands over me yammering about first aid, Larry distracts Mom by climbing out of his high chair. "Give yourself a minute, Hattie." She rushes off to catch him before he falls on his head.

I try nodding, but I don't think my head moves. I close my eyes and focus on breathing. Taking in air makes me feel better than anything, and as long as Mom is busy, I'll take the time to recover.

"What happened?" I whisper to Beverly.

"I think you fainted," she says. "You know...from the shock."

Beverly gazes at Crackers and says something, I can't make out what, but Crackers crouches on the floor next to me in an instant. "Don't worry, Hattie. We'll figure this out. No problem is too great for the Dream Girls."

Crackers is like medicine sometimes.

The girls help me up from the floor and I stand, all wobbly, sinking against the counter and trying to force my legs to hold me up.

"We'll go down and clean up our mess, Mom," Crackers

says. "Hattie's fine. Just a little woozy."

Mom peers at me, concerned etched across her brow. "Hattie? Are you sure you're feeling better?"

I fake a smile. "Sure," I manage.

I count the seventeen steps out of the kitchen and then Crackers lifts my arm around her shoulders before she helps me downstairs. Beverly follows, faithfully peering over her shoulder to make sure Mom isn't on our tail.

Once we make our way to the basement, Crackers sits me in one of the folding chairs and instructs me to put my head between my knees. "When you keep your head down, the blood goes to your brain, so synapses can start firing again. I've seen my dad do it a zillion times when he feels dizzy, and in a jiffy he's up and back to normal."

Crackers. Knows. Everything.

Before too long, my head stops the constant throbbing, but thumps a little every few minutes, like a big bass drum in a orchestra. Boom. Boom. Boom. Then nothing.

"Better?" Beverly narrows her eyes and bites her lips. She's a bit of a worrier, like me.

I blink a few times, bringing the collage we taped on the wall last night into focus. "Much."

"For a minute there, you had us worried, Hattie girl. But now, instead of looking like Casper the ghost, you look like a pale white girl again." Crackers wallops her knee, proud of her joke.

I roll my eyes. Beverly too. Crackers thinks she's funnier than Carol Burnett.

"Isn't it weird that we turn white when we pass out?" She swings around and points a finger at Beverly. "When you go into shock, like you did after you read the horrid note Mrs.

Simmons wrote, you turned gray."

"We say ashy," Beverly corrects.

Crackers glues a finger to her lips and cocks her head. "Fine, you get ashy."

I giggle at my friends. They're a sideshow.

"Do you still want to go to the park?" Beverly asks.

"For sure." Nothing will keep me from spending time with my friends.

We fold our sleeping bags, gather our Coke bottles and snack dishes and Crackers runs them up to the kitchen, then we all get dressed.

As soon as we start a table hockey tournament, Mom calls downstairs, "Girls, the bus leaves in fifteen minutes. Start bundling up." Thank goodness, Crackers hasn't given up a game yet, or she'd be impossible to deal with.

"Good thing you have a station wagon." Beverly wraps and tucks a scarf around her neck and stuffs the extra fabric inside her jacket. "There's plenty of room for all of us."

Crackers hikes up her snow pants and elbows Beverly in the ribs. "You're so teensie we could stuff you in the glove box if we had too."

"Let's get upstairs before my brothers," I say. "They love sitting all the way in the back, but if we get there first, we'll call dibs."

Crackers closes one eye, her Pirate stare, and aims a finger at me. "Hattie, I don't care what anyone says about you, you're one smart cookie."

We mash each other into the stairwell, race up the steps, yank our boots over our shoes, and shove each other out the door and down the driveway. Dad's revving the car engine, just like always. Patience is a virtue, and when God was passing out assets, my dad must have been late to the distribution party.

I undo the latch on the rear door, tip up the window glass and we climb in. Snuggling together in "the way back," as we call it, we hold hands and sing *Stop in the Name of Love*, finally letting go of each other and acting out the song, just like The Supremes.

By the time we reach Rouge Park and tote the toboggan up the hill, I've completely forgotten the shocking news that I've been admitted to St. Mary's.

CHAPTER TWO

THE NEXT MORNING, THE THROBBING IN MY HEAD IS back. I thought my new glasses would help, but my headaches haven't disappeared yet. Even rolling over and pulling my pillow over my head doesn't help. Especially when fate creeps back into my awareness. Me. A Catholic school kid again. My stomach twists into a gigantic knot.

I sit up in bed and rub my eyes, hoping the news is part of a terrible nightmare, but in the back of my mind, I know better. I hang my legs over the side of my bed and swing them, watching my feet sway back and forth, thinking as hard as I can.

Dad taught me to stay between the lines, which means following the rules, as close as I can anyway, and I remember the lesson, practically curling into a ball as I lay back down. Soon though, Dr. King's words play in my head. In the letter he sent me, he said I was courageous. He said I wasn't alone. He said we would raise our voices together. Recalling his words makes me brave. I can do this. I can overcome.

I jerk on pants and a shirt and march downstairs, my shoulders squared and fierce determination set in my eyes. I know because I rehearsed in the mirror after I got dressed. Mom and Dad are right where I expect to find them, in the kitchen, sipping coffee at the table. Larry palms Cheerios while he hangs out in his high chair, and I kiss his head before sitting down and folding my hands on the table. "I want to talk to you guys about St. Mary's. I know how you much you want me to go to school there, but I'd like you to hear what I have to say, then maybe we can compromise." Dad mentions "compromising" all the time when my brothers and I disagree. Maybe he'll like how I thought about a solution to our problem. My problem, that is.

Mom and Dad pass a knowing look between them, arching their brows, and then focus back on me. A quiver of nervousness zips through my arms. I swallow hard and think again of Dr. King's words, reminding myself to be courageous.

I suck in a deep breath and begin. "I never thought I'd like Crary better than Catholic school. But I've made the best friends I've ever had in my life since public school. Plus, we're just getting started making a difference in the world. I won the essay contest and Martin Luther King, Jr. wrote me a letter. He said I'm helping, fighting for the rights of all the people. So, I'm doing great at Crary. At Catholic school, I'll just be one of the soldiers. I know, a soldier of Christ, but kids are all the same there. No one is encouraged to be different, or to achieve their dreams."

"Who inspires you at Crary?" Dad interrupts.

He poses a good question. I squeeze my eyes shut tight for a minute and purse my lips.

"Maxine, Timmy, Joey, Mrs. Simmons—all the people who don't want blacks and whites to be friends. They inspire me to change their minds. To show them how we're all the same inside. Beverly loves her mom and dad as much as I love you. She's as smart as anyone I know. Crackers proves everyday how girls can be as athletic as boys and she teaches me not to be afraid. Back when I was a Catholic school kid, I was always afraid—paralyzed, like my feet were cemented to the ground. Sometimes I could barely move, or speak, or breathe. Now I know better. I'm as capable as any boy, or genius, or beautiful model in Seventeen magazine.

"I can make a difference in the world, and I want to. Starting now, not after I'm an adult, but while I'm ten. Bet you no black students attend St. Mary's. Beverly is my friend. Crackers is my friend. I'm better with them than I've ever been. They make me the best person I can be."

I lean back and wait, pretty sure I've built a solid case, like Perry Mason on TV. Even though I hadn't planned exactly every word I wanted to say, or talking for all that time, my parents have to be impressed.

Dad's eyes narrow—his thinking-things-over face.

Mom sinks against the back of her chair and crosses her arms. She's been my fiercest opponent at times in the past. If I make her mad, she'll be impossible to reason with.

I start to shake, just a little tremor at first. But within seconds, my knees knock together under the table and goosebumps pepper my arms. Who am I to tell my parents what I'm going to do?

Crackers' voice whispers in my ear, "Good job, Hattie. You got their attention."

Mom and Dad pass an understanding glance between them and I catch a hint of agreement in Mom's expression when she nods ever so slightly and uncrosses her arms, then in Dad's eyes when he arches his brows a bit, as if he is surprised how well I argued my point.

He shouldn't be surprised. As the head of his debate team in high school, he knows where that spark comes from. Heredity.

Dad grips Mom's hand as he locks eyes with me. "I'm proud of all you've done this year, Hattie, and I must admit, you've surprised me today. But I shouldn't be at all shocked. You're turning out just like Mom and I expected. We want you to be an independent thinker, but what you're asking is far outside anything we ever dreamed for you. We're going to need to think about this. As you know, time is short. We only have three more days before the end of vacation, and you're expected at St. Mary's Tuesday morning. Are you sure you don't want to go to school with Colleen?"

Colleen is my Catholic friend from down the street. I love her, I really do, but she isn't Beverly, and for sure she isn't Crackers. I want to stay at Crary.

I lock eyes with him for a minute, then I fix my gaze on Mom and say with more fire in my heart than ever before, "Positive."

"We'll get back to you."

CHAPTER THREE

A T FIRST, THERE'S A LIGHTNESS IN MY STEP, LIKE I'M walking on cotton candy, but once I hit the stairs, my legs grow as heavy as pylons. What if my parents say no? My heart sinks at the thought. How will I ever tell Crackers and Beverly I'm not coming back to Crary?

Now I know what losing a limb feels like, except if I lose my two best friends, I'll be without both my arms and both my legs. Limbless. Mom's familiar words echo in my brain—stop the pity party, Hattie.

Slumping against the wall, closing my eyes and pressing my palms together, I point my fingers straight to the sky. I pray, making a deal with God. "If you let me stay at Crary, I promise I will never be mean to my brothers again. I'll help more around the house, and never lie or disobey my parents." The promise is a fib, and I know better.

I try a different tack.

"God, please do the right thing."

Then, I rethink my prayer. God probably wants me to go to a Catholic school.

If only I could talk to Crackers or Beverly right now. Or my Grandma. Or Martin Luther King, Jr. They would know what to do.

This bravery thing is heaps harder than I ever imagined.

An idea fires through my brain. If I perch on the landing, I might be able to eavesdrop on Mom and Dad. Tiptoeing over to the staircase, I make my way down the four steps to the landing and slip into the far corner. If Dad or Mom starts to come upstairs, I can sneak back to my room before they spot me.

At first their voices are low, murmurs I can't make out. I squint, because for some reason, I concentrate better when I narrow my eyes. After a few seconds, I catch some of their words.

"On the other hand, we can't let Hattie make the rules. Plus, if she continues at Crary we have to figure out a way to drive her to catechism each week."

"I've already been taking her," Dad said. "That's not an issue."

Just as I guessed, Dad is on my side. Mom isn't.

"Part of me wants this for her," Mom says. "Our girl has more gumption than I have in my baby toe."

"Don't sell yourself short, honey. You've raised a spunky girl. She's a lot like her mom."

I imagine Dad winking when he says that, because he does think Mom is bold and determined. For the first time, I realize how alike Mom and I are. Maybe we clash because we have the same personality. The thought makes me shiver.

"She's made a huge difference at Crary. Pulling her out now might give the wrong impression. Hattie and her friends made a mark, and that diversity lesson they came up with was pure genius. Think about it. Hattie wins an essay contest about friendship without boundaries, then she doesn't return to school. How will that look?" Dad says.

"We can't make a decision about our daughter's future based on appearances."

Mom's words confuse me. When we moved to our new house and I wanted to be friends with Beverly, she was totally worried about what the neighbors would say if I had a black friend.

"I agree, Joan, but we have to consider all the angles."

"Yes," Mom says. "I suppose you're right."

A long silence follows, and I squeeze my eyes shut and make a wish, in case I have a fairly godmother I don't know about. "Crary. Crary. Crary."

"I hate being rushed to make a decision this important," Dad says.

"I always thought our kids would all attend the same school."

"The plan has always been for Hattie to attend St. Mary's for the sixth grade. Maybe we stick to the blueprint, and tell Hattie we will allow her to stay at Crary for fifth grade, but she'll attend St. Mary's as scheduled for the sixth. Then we have time to make a decision about what's best."

"Great idea!" Mom's voice lifts with relief.

"We can tell her in a few hours. Make sure we're still comfortable with our decision."

A grin grows across my face and the vice squeezing my heart releases. I can breathe again. I cross my fingers and toes for a full thirty seconds, then creep upstairs to my room and make my bed. For good measure, I cross my eyes. Wishes can come true.

A huge weight lifts, yet I still have this knot in my belly. They could change their minds.

Matt knocks on my bedroom door. "Want to play hockey?"

Matt likes Crackers, and he has more respect for me since I've been hanging out with her. Like he believes I could play some sports now. In secret, I think he might have a crush on her.

All the boys at school do. Not only is she good at basketball, but when winter came and the ball wouldn't bounce on the pavement, they started playing football at recess, and waited for Crackers to get outside before they picked teams. Everyone wanted her on their team. She throws the ball better than any of the boys and is speedier than the cartoon Road Runner. Crackers is a flash.

She could be the first woman in the NFL, if she doesn't make the NBA first.

A fierce, howling wind blows against my door. Almost like an omen. Something bad is about to happen. If only I weren't so superstitious.

"Hattie?" Matt says.

"Sorry, I was thinking about something."

"What? What's going on?"

I'm not about to tell him. He'll have an opinion that he's not afraid to share. He teased me about going to public school, and how I'd wind up dumb as a rock because I wasn't getting a prime education at a Catholic school, but the truth is, he wishes he could be at Crary, where they have a band for fifth graders. He wants to be a musician when he grows up, like James Taylor,

Elton John, or Paul McCartney.

"Nothing's wrong. Let's go play."

He beats me three games to none. A shut out.

Guess I need more lessons with Crackers.

Dad calls me to the kitchen when we are about to start the fourth game.

The nerves in my stomach jumble up, and I tell Matt, "Be right back."

I hurry up the steps and perch on the edge of a chair across from Mom and Dad, trying to wipe the smirk off my face. The sun shines like a thousand lights, the aroma of baked chicken fills the room. Nothing can go wrong on such a perfect day.

"Hattie," Dad says, his brows knitting. "Mom and I have talked this over. There are quite a few issues to consider, and we've taken some time to discuss them and to sit with our decision for a bit before talking to you."

Yes. Yes. I know the drill, Dad. This isn't the first time we've talked about something serious. Just tell me.

"We want you to give St. Mary's a try."

My throat fills with dread. "What? But how? Why?" I choke out the words. "I thought…"

"We know this is hard news, Hattie, but as parents we're obligated to make the best decision. For you and for our family. We know how much you'll miss your friends, but you already know Colleen, and we can still do overnights and visits with your friends from Crary."

"They aren't just friends from Crary." My voice rises, even though I know better than to talk back to my parents. "They're my family. They're my life."

The thought of Crackers and Beverly being alone together—without me—makes me want to crawl into a cave and die.

They'll be happy. A fierce twosome. No more Dream Girls. Just the two of them, arm in arm, playing handclaps and winning spelling bees and getting the best grades in the class. Without me.

"I hope you're happy!" I shout. "You just ruined my life."

I storm up to my room and slam the door. Tears rush like a river. If I could, I'd turn back time and be nine forever. I climb under my covers and cry my eyes out.

Later, a soft knock sounds on my bedroom door.

"Go away!"

"It's me," Matt says. "Can I come in?"

I sit up in bed and blow my nose. "Yes."

Matt slips inside and closes the door behind him. "I'm sorry, Hattie. I came upstairs when I heard you shouting and I eavesdropped on Mom and Dad after you stomped out of the kitchen. Can I do anything?"

I wrap my arms around his neck and sob. "How can they do this to me? Don't they care about me at all?"

Matt backs me away and locks my gaze. "They're parents, Hattie. Haven't you figured them out yet?"

I collapse back on my pillow, wipe my eyes, and peer at him. "What do you mean?"

"There are times you can get around them and times you can't. This is one of the times you can't. But you don't have to do well at St. Mary's. You can fail at everything, then they'll have to put you back at Crary."

"I'm not like you. I can't do things just to have my own way."

He straightens his shoulders, more than normal. "Think about this, Hattie. What would Crackers tell you to do?"

"How do you know what Crackers would do?"

"You think I'm just your dumb little brother, but I'm way smarter than you think. Crackers would tell you exactly what I'm telling you. Do something to make this work for you. Adults have been telling us what to do our entire lives. Me, I figured out early how to get around them."

"You're only nine. I don't know how you learned this already." I'm feeling pretty stupid right now, I think it's actually called naïve, but I'm not admitting that to him.

"Hattie," he says with a disgusted sigh, "from the time I was two, I've been able to wrap Mom around my baby finger. If I cried and threw a tantrum, she gave me my way. Now, I do things behind her back or just ignore her. It's no big deal. You worry she won't love you anymore, but not me. She has to love us. She's our mom. "

"I'm not conniving. I could never do those things. Plus, I tried. I went to Crackers' house that one time without telling and Mom and Dad found out. I hate making them unhappy, and whenever I do the wrong thing, I feel guilty."

Matt chews his cheek as he narrows his eyes. "You'll never survive."

"If I go to St. Mary's and don't do my work, Mom and Dad will punish me. They know I'm a good student, even if I am distracted sometimes."

"Just don't show up. When Mom makes sure Eddie is going to walk with us Monday, we can tell her now that our big sister goes to St. Mary's, we don't need to meet up with him." Eddie's older—a 6th grader from the neighborhood—so Mom trusts him to walk with my brothers.

Matt elbows me in the side, grabs my pillow and hits me over the head. "Then…"

My brain races. I could go to Crary as usual, and the boys

could walk to St. Mary's. They can walk by themselves. They're old enough. This might work.

"Maybe," I say. "Just maybe."

CHAPTER FOUR

I GET SUPER LUCKY THAT NIGHT. MOM AND DAD GO TO THE neighbors' to play bridge, so I'm home alone with my brothers. Johnny and Larry are already tucked in bed and sound asleep, so just Robert and Matt and I are awake. I slip out of the den where they are spread out on the floor, thoroughly engrossed in watching Gunsmoke, and tiptoe upstairs to use the phone.

I could call Beverly first, but she'll tell me I have to do what my parents say, and besides, so close to eight o'clock, her mother might think calling after dark is too late. I'll call Crackers. She's probably home alone anyway, being the weekend and all. Her dad spends a lot of time at the bar with his friends.

I huddle on the carpet and dial her number. If Matt or Robert spot me on the phone, they might tell Mom and Dad, and then questions will come—ones I don't want to answer.

I'm clenching my teeth, saying a silent prayer. The phone rings four times before Crackers answers, "Hello!"

"Hey."

"Hattie? What's wrong?"

I bite my lip, wrapping the phone cord tighter around my index finger, fighting back tears. Crackers wouldn't cry if this happened to her. She'd just make a plan, end of story. I square my shoulders, feigning I'm unafraid like she would be, and lay out the problem.

"My parents are making me go to St. Mary's. I thought I could talk them out of it, but no luck."

"What?" Crackers sounds shocked. That's never a good sign.

"You heard me. Somebody moved after the riots, so there's a spot open in 5th grade. My parents think it's divine intervention, like God made this happen. Mom and Dad say I have to go, even though I told them Crary is way better than Catholic school and how I can't live without you and Beverly."

"Tsk, tsk, tsk," Crackers says. "This one's a conundrum."

I sidle up against my parent's bed and relax for a minute. Crackers has a way of making me feel lighter. "You love that word, don't you?"

Crackers laughs. "What's that...when you say words that sound like what they mean?"

"Onomatopoeia."

She laughs again.

Now she's getting off track and I can't afford to waste time. "This isn't time for fun and games. I have a serious problem."

"I'm thinking, Hattie. I know it might surprise you, but once in a while, I have to think."

"So, you agree," I say.

"This qualifies as a big problem." Crackers goes quiet.

"What am I going to do?"

"We can't change your parents' mind, so whose can we change? What about Mrs. Simmons', or the principal's? Mrs. Foster loves us, and she went nutty over our experiment and what we did in class. Maybe we can talk to her, and convince her to tell your parents they're making a huge mistake. She might be able to persuade them."

A long silence follows. Just the TV downstairs hums in the background. The normal cozy, warm, comforting feeling I have when I'm snuggled up next to my parents' bed turns to an arctic chill.

"I have an idea!"

"Is this one good?" I'm worried there's no hope.

"All my ideas are good, Hattie."

"Tell me."

"I will if you'll be quiet. We need to buy some time. Try to get your parents to let you come back to Crary for just a few days after break. The semester ends the last of January. Maybe they will let you wait until then to switch, and by that time, we'll have a plan."

The room warms up in a flash. "Good idea. I need to finish the term so I can get my grades, turn in my books, and say goodbye to my friends. At least that's what I'll pretend, but we'll have to come up with a plan, and fast. I'll talk to my parents in the morning. Right after church when they're feeling particularly full of Grace."

"Nice one, Hattie."

A wave of relief washes over me.

Calling Crackers was the best idea! After I hang up the phone, I peek outside and zero in on the North Star. "I wish I may, I wish I might…"

When we come home from church the following Sunday, I help Mom in the kitchen. She's cheerful, singing along to some tunes on the radio as the kitchen fills with the smell of sizzling bacon and melting butter. The sun streams through the window, and birds sing, making noise like spring might be right around the corner, but no, it's just the January thaw. Still, my heart sucks in the strength of the light as I crack eggs into a bowl, pour in a bit of milk and scramble them.

"I have a giant favor to ask." I try to keep my tone casual, as if I'm asking her to pass me the salt.

"What's that?"

I pull in a deep breath for courage and blurt out, "Can I please, please, please go to Crary until the end of the semester? I'm doing so well in my classes—I think I'm getting all A's. But we have some big exams coming up in two weeks, and they're part of my grade. Plus, I have to turn in my textbooks and say goodbye to my teacher and my friends."

Mom tightens her lips into a thin line. "Going to your new school won't mean you can't keep your friends, Hattie. Plus, St. Mary's has a waiting list. They won't hold your spot open."

Maybe I can guilt her into waiting. "But when we moved away from the old neighborhood, I never saw Joanne or Mary again. You promised I would, but I haven't."

Mom's eyes mist over and a pang hits my heart. I want to say, *All right, I'll go to St. Mary's,* but I can't.

She bites her lip, and steam builds up in her chest. "I can return your textbooks and collect your belongings from Crary. Schools are accustomed to students moving out and starting new schools between semesters. We've made our minds up,

Hattie."

"Could you promise to talk to Dad before you give me an answer?" Dad will like my idea. He's a teacher. He'll understand.

Mom spins away and drops a glass. It shatters to smithereens. For some reason, I think this is my fault.

I dart to the closet to get the broom and dustpan. "Stay out of the kitchen. We broke a glass," I warn my brothers.

I rush back to sweep up the shards of glass. Mom leans on the counter, her hands slayed over her face. When I'm done checking the floor for slivers, I toss the remnants in the trash, and give Mom a hug. "Everything's going to be okay, Mom."

Mom holds on tight and says, "Yes, Hattie girl, I know."

I force down a few bites of breakfast—I'm about to face a prison sentence. My appetite disappeared with Mom's dictate. My head begins to pound.

After finishing the dishes, I escape to my bedroom. The room is beautiful. Mom painted the walls lavender and bought me the flowery bedspread of my dreams, with a matching eyelet dust ruffle. I should be happy. I should be grateful. I slink over to my bookcase and pull out Black Beauty. Although I'm reading about a horse, the story is really about hardship. Black Beauty is real to me, a person who's been through so much. Like me, and Beverly, and Crackers.

I read the same sentence a dozen times. Times like this, action suits me better. I race downstairs and call into the kitchen.

"Be right back. I'm running to Colleen's."

This will make Mom happy. She'll think I'm going to deliver the good news to my Catholic school friend, but I'm really coming up with a list of possibilities. Ways out of St. Mary's.

I zip down the street and call out, "Colleen!" at the back door. Her mom opens the door and stares at me.

"Hattie," she says in a disapproving voice, her lips forming a stiff line after she says my name. Her eyes narrow and she steps back, as if she can't decide whether to invite me in or not, but she eases out of the doorway after an uncomfortably long minute, and calls Colleen. Mrs. Baldo is nervous because I'm a public school kid. She's afraid I'll have a bad influence on Colleen. She never said so, but it's how Catholics act around public school kids. I know because my mom used to act the same way.

"Hattie's here," she says as she turns her back on me.

Uneasiness takes hold of my feet and I can't make them move. Thankfully, Colleen bounds into the room and smiles. "Did you have a good Christmas? Come see what I got."

Colleen's parents have fewer kids than mine, just her and an older sister, so they always have way more toys and clothes than me. I don't mind, but I can't help but notice. Sometimes I wonder what it would like to be rich.

I follow her upstairs. Their house always smells like flowers, which I guess can happen when you don't have a troop of little boys filling the air with sweaty heads. It's beautiful here too, and I dream that one day I'll have a pink-canopied bed like Colleen with pearly white shag carpet on the floor. Colleen pulls out a vinyl box from her closet. It says "Barbie Family House" on the front and has a shiny gold clasp, which she unfastens. I watch with bated breath. Inside the house, Colleen lets down a floor and unfolds the walls. The cardboard partitions are painted to look like a living room, bedroom, and kitchen, modern and cheerful. The kitchen area has checkerboard walls with a hot pink awning. "It's amazing, Colleen. How did you ever get this? I haven't even seen one before!"

"My dad was able to get it before the official release. It's not coming out until April. Working for J.L. Hudson has its advantages."

"You are so lucky!"

I've wanted the Barbie house that came out five years ago, but my wish never came true.

"We can play if you want. Go home and get your Barbie."

"That's okay." I don't want to have fun today. I want to figure out how to convince Mom to let me go back to Crary. "I don't have much time."

I can't bring myself to tell Colleen the news that I'll be her classmate in two days. If I say the words aloud, that makes the move real, and I'm not ready to make my future official. I hope beyond hope I can change things.

"So," I mention as I twist the carpet threads in my fingers, "how's school going? Do you like your teacher?"

Colleen gives me a puzzled look before she grabs a book off her bookcase and leafs through it. "Sister Theresa? She's okay. Kind of strict, but what else is new?"

"Do you have any black kids at school?"

She stops and locks eyes with me. "Are you obsessed with black kids?"

"No, why do you ask?" I straighten my shoulders and anger chokes my throat. Why can't Colleen see that skin color doesn't matter?

"Every time I see you, you want to know something about Negroes."

I shrug, trying to act nonchalant. "Just curious is all."

"Don't get crazy about civil rights. It's a passing thing."

My heart clenches in my chest. I hope she's wrong. "What are you learning? Have you started reciprocals yet?"

"Oh, we're way past that. We're even doing some geometry now."

Great. I'm going to be so far behind. I'd always thought Catholic schools were way better than public, and it's true. Or maybe they are just teaching things out of order. Maybe I'm jumping to conclusions. How can I use this to convince my parents I should stay at Crary?

"What about kids in class? Are they all well behaved? Any problem kids?"

"What's wrong with you, Hattie? Since when do you care about what's going on at St. Mary's?"

I turn my eyes to the floor. "No reason."

"I got a Ouija board too."

The idea of asking the Ouija board a question or two sends a jolt of electricity up my spine. "Can I call home and see if Mom will let me stay for a bit so we can try out the board?"

"Sure."

I step into the hall and call home. The Baldo's have this cool little cave in their wall where the telephone sits. I feel so grownup when I use this phone. And more confident. Mom agrees to let me play at Colleen's for an hour. Plenty of time.

When I step back inside Colleen's room, she has drawn the shades and made the room as dark as possible. Using a Ouija board at night is best, when the spirits are more alive and daily life interferes less with the spirit world, but this is super close. The board and planchette, or pointer, are on a black cloth on the floor. Colleen loves to set the mood for everything we do.

I know exactly what question to ask the board, and vow not to lead the magic circle to the answer I long to see.

"You go first," I say. The owner of the game always goes first. Our unspoken rule.

A smile curls on Colleen's lips and she lightly places her fingertips on the edge of the planchette, then closes her eyes.

I do the same. Unsure how we'll see the answers, I peek once I feel the pointer move.

"Does Patrick like me as much as I like him?"

Colleen told me about Patrick before. He has the bluest eyes she's ever seen and she thinks he's Scandinavian because his blond hair is almost white. Since Colleen's hair is blonde too, and naturally curly, she thinks they would have beautiful children.

The pointer starts moving, guiding our hands with the force of a high-powered magnet. We don't help at all. Energy zips through the air, so much so that I'm a little spooked. Before I can blink, the planchette stops. In the dim light, I see Colleen open her eyes. She must like to start playing with her eyes shut. Another way for her to set the mood.

Just as she hoped, the magic circle lands over the "Yes" on the board, right next to the drawing of the sun. "See?" I whisper. "What you've always wanted."

"Your turn," she says.

The urge is so powerful, I can't wait a minute longer. "Promise to close your eyes. And no comments on my question, okay?"

"Sure, Hattie. Whatever you say."

A hush settles over the room, and I wait a full minute before speaking.

"Will I…" I hold my breath for three solid seconds before I speak again. "…be happy at St. Mary's?"

Colleen stays quiet. I expect her to gasp when she hears my question, but she keeps her promise.

The magic circle moves beneath our touch. I am dying to open my eyes, but if I sway the answer, I'll never know the truth. After what seems like an eternity, the planchette stops moving. I dare to open my eyes.

Colleen locks eyes with me. Just as I'd expected. The magic circle encases the word "No" next to the moon.

My heart pounds, right before it sinks like a stone.

"Everything will be okay, Hattie. Just you wait and see."

My lip quivers. I will not cry in front of Colleen. I will not shed a single tear. Grandma says things happen for a reason. I'll be as brave as I've ever been.

Wait. I don't even have a uniform.

"Colleen," I say. "Would you understand if I went home now?"

She rests a gentle hand on my shoulder. "Sure." I put on my coat and trudge down the street, my heart weighing two tons. Maybe three. I swear it's already sunk to my toes.

Inside the back hall, I hang up my coat and slip off my boots, not caring that my shoes come off inside them, and slip inside the half bath and hug my arms around my knees, huddling on the floor. Being brave is still new to me, but I summon every ounce of courage, splash my face with cold water and go to talk to Mom.

She's in the kitchen, baking brownies. Quiet blankets the rest of the house.

"Where are Dad and the boys?"

"Larry is down for a nap and Dad took the boys to school with him. He has some lesson plans to write and the boys wanted to play in the band room while he works, so they're out of our hair for a while."

"Can I talk to you?"

"Of course, Hattie. What's on your mind?"

How she doesn't know about knocks me over, but sometimes Mom uses this as a tactic, pretending she has no idea what's bothering me.

"I know things happen for a reason, and I'm guessing I got into St. Mary's because I'm meant to go there. I also understand they won't hold my spot forever. Here's the thing though. I don't even have a uniform. You know what it's like to stick out like a sore thumb. You know how I hate being the center of attention. I can't even stand for people to notice my glasses. I'm enough of a misfit all on my own. Could we please wait just a day or two until I have the same clothes as everyone else?"

"I asked Sr. Mary George about that. She said you could just wear a navy blue skirt and a white blouse until your uniform arrives. Students often wear the same outfit when they first start school there. No problem at all, honey. You won't stand out."

A knot of dread fills me. Postponing the inevitable isn't working. "Okay."

"Perk up, Hattie. Going to St. Mary's will be an adjustment, but Colleen will be there with you, along with the boys."

I close my eyes. My head feels like a knife is slicing through my brain.

"I do have some good news for you. Since it's New Year's Eve, Grandma is coming to fix dinner and spend the night."

My heart does a flip. Grandma. My prayers are answered. Finally.

CHAPTER FIVE

W HEN GRANDMA WALKS THROUGH THE DOOR WITH
a roaster pan, the scent of pot roast, potatoes,
carrots, onions, and gravy make my stomach
rumble, an audible growl riding on its tail. She hands me the
pot, careful to make sure I have a firm grip of the oven mitts as
I take the dish from her, and place it on top of the stove, turn on
the oven to warm, and slide the pot inside.

Mom and Grandma chat in the front hall while she removes her gloves and boots, and Dad takes her coat and hangs
it in the front hall closet. "You two have a good time," she says,
kissing both their cheeks. "And if you need a ride home, call. I
can leave Hattie with the kids for a few minutes. I don't want
you driving if you have too much to drink."

"Thanks for the offer, Genevieve, but I think we'll be fine."

"In any case, call if you need me."

I tiptoe into the dining room to catch of glimpse of Mom
from the hallway, hoping she will say something to my grand-

mother about my news—I'm expected at St. Mary's in two days.

Mom slides on her high heels and Dad drapes her fox fur around her shoulders. "Doesn't my wife look beautiful?"

"She's a vision," Grandma says as she lays a hand on Mom's shoulder and kisses her on the cheek one more time. Mom does look stunning. She's wearing my favorite dress, a chiffon print with splashy turquoise flowers and spaghetti straps. Her eyes shine like copper pennies.

The boys tromp down the stairs before anything more is said.

"Grandma's here! Woo-hoo! Want to play war, Grandma?"

Grandma throws her head back. Her laugh, the heartiest of any I've ever heard, echoes up the stairwell. "Maybe after dinner, but only if I'm on the winning side."

"You will be," Rob says, holding out a green plastic army man. "Here, this guy always wins."

"Let me check on the roast first. Would you like to set the table, Matt, or is it your turn, Hattie?"

"I can set it, Matt."

Matt's face lights up like I've just handed him a bag of penny candy. "Thanks, Hattie."

I want to act cool and nonchalant, but the likelihood of remaining calm in the middle of the worst crisis of my life is zero. Zilch. Nada. Grandma strolls into the kitchen, and I about knock her down, I trail so close on her heels.

"Grandma, I need to talk to you."

"Hattie, settle yourself. Let me put the water on for tea. Care to join me?"

With a hefty dose of milk and two sugar cubes, maybe. She rests her hand on my shoulder. "Count to ten," she says, "and don't forget to breathe."

"I know you say everything happens for a reason, but this time, I'm not sure I agree, and I know you believe in action, not just sitting back letting the world spin around you. So, when Mom told me I was admitted to St. Mary's and start the day after tomorrow, I thought of everything—excuses, lies, even logical reasons why I should stay at Crary, but nothing's worked. Do you have any ideas? Please?"

The kettle whistles from the stove and Grandma busies herself pulling out the teacups she'd passed on to Mom from her mother. While her family had been dirt poor growing up, as she said, my great grandmother, Hattie, whom I was named after, did have a few nice things when she was older.

My favorite is the gold-gilded fluted cup, painted black with a blossoming pink rose on the front. Grandma chooses another black cup, but her favorite has fully opened white roses. They are so much alike, I call them sister cups.

Grandma pours the boiling water into each cup, then places a tea bag in each to steep. There's no hurrying her along, so I fill the creamer with milk and set the sugar bowl on the table, along with two spoons and napkins. My heartbeat slows to a trot and by the time we sit down, my pulse might be back to normal.

"Let's think this through," Grandma says as she perches on a chair and takes my hand, brushing a stray lock of hair off my cheek with the other. "Nothing gets accomplished with reactions."

A ragged breath comes out when I try to talk. Grandma knows me better than anyone, and I respect her more than any person on planet Earth. She's wise, loves me even when I'm horrid, and believes in me.

"It's just that Crary has become like home to me. And

Crackers and Beverly Jo are the sisters I never had."

Grandma raises her eyebrows, almost like she knows something I don't. Is Mom pregnant? I make a mental note to check her middle. Mom has a trim figure, so she could disguise things like another baby brother pretty easily by wearing a fuller top.

"Have a sip of tea, Hattie."

Grandma purses her lips and leans back in her chair. "You remember the last time I interfered with your mother's plans, don't you?"

Boy, do I. I thought World War III was going to break out in the kitchen.

"I don't want you to do anything to interfere, just give me some advice. You're smarter than me. You know what I should do!"

"I can't tell you what to do, Hattie, but consider this. You're nervous and scared, just like before you went to Crary. But you have the experience behind you now, which means you're stronger than you were a few months ago. Consider what you accomplished at Crary. The lesson you taught your class and your winning essay. You have so much to be proud of, and you'll be an asset to the fifth grade class at St. Mary's.

"I'm sure your teacher will want you to share the experience with the class. You can start a new Dream Girls group at St. Mary's."

"But I don't want to grow our group. I want Beverly and Crackers and me to be the members. The only members."

"Think about Dr. King. He could have stayed in his comfort zone, too, couldn't he? He could have decided he was too frightened to spread his message, decided not to put his life on the line. Warriors don't hide, they stick out their noses, and they fight for what they believe in. You can fight for equality at St. Mary's where the struggle is much more difficult for people to understand. They hide behind the safety of the Church, the insulated community, and giving gifts to the poor, rather than including them. There is so much you could do to heighten their awareness."

My stomach sinks to my knees. "You really don't have an idea how I can stay at Crary?"

Matt marches into the kitchen. "Haven't you figured this out this yet?"

I scowl and glare at him. Couldn't he keep this between us? If Grandma knows we're scheming, she can't play dumb if I decide to use any of his ideas. Not like any of his hijinks are reasonable.

"Smells good in here. What time's dinner?"

Grandma's eyes twinkle when her mouth curls up in a grin. "Food's ready. We can eat whenever you like."

I hop up from the table and begin to gather dishes from the cupboard. Dinner makes for a perfect distraction. I'll have to plot my plan later. By myself.

CHAPTER SIX

MOM'S STERN VOICE AWAKENS ME TWO MORNINGS later. "Hattie, hurry up. Did you forget to set your alarm? You're going to be late for your first day at St. Mary's."

With a start, I rub the sleep from my eyes, trying to clear my vision. Everything is shady, like I'm inside a cloud where grays go from dim to black. Maybe I'm dreaming, and it's still night. I peer at the window, searching for daylight behind the shade. When I can't find the sun, even when I squint, I check the clock, reaching for my nightstand and turning the dial in my direction. I can't read a thing. Can't even see the hands of the clock. They are supposed to illuminate in a dark room.

I grab my glasses and wrap them around my ears, blinking again. Since Dad and I picked them up from the optician, they seemed to be helping. The headaches pretty much disappeared. But now? Nothing but darkness.

"Mom!" I cry. "Come here! Please!"

"I'm changing the baby's diaper. What is it?"

"I can't see."

Panic closes my throat, and I try to imagine what's happening. Maybe if I just lie back on my pillow for a minute and blink a few more times. My heart races like a jackrabbit, and I stumble out of bed.

"Mom, I need you. It's an emergency!"

I reach out my hands, feeling my way in the dark, and step forward ever so slowly, shuffling my feet on the floor so I don't bump into anything. Tears start running down my face without my realizing, but at last I find my bedroom door and hang onto the knob for dear life.

"What's wrong with you?" Matt asks. "Why aren't you dressed yet?"

"I can't see," I choke out. "I can't see."

"Good one, Hattie," he whispers, "but Mom won't fall for a ridiculous excuse. Lame idea. Try something else, something more realistic. Want me to get the heating pad? You can warm your head for a few minutes and say you have a fever. Quick, go in the bathroom and lock the door. I'll bring you the pad."

"I'm not kidding, I can't see!" I wave my hand in front of my face. "Where are you? Give me your hand and take me to Mom."

"Knock it off. You're a bad actress."

I slump to the floor, hang my head in my hands, and start to wail.

"Okay, fine. I'll get Mom."

His footsteps drag as he walks away. I struggle to catch my breath, but snot clogs my throat.

"What on earth?" Mom's voice.

I try swallowing to calm down, but nothing seems to help.

"I can't see. I woke up and thought maybe I had a bad dream and it wasn't morning yet, but everyone is getting ready for school."

Mom rests a hand on my shoulder and crouches down in front of me. "What do you mean?"

"Everything is shadowy. Like in a haunted house or something. I can hear you, but no matter how hard I try, I can't see. I'm not lying. I'm not trying to get out of going to St. Mary's, if that's what you're thinking. I can't see."

A river of tears flows down my face.

"Get your sister a tissue," Mom tells Matt.

Matt's footfalls trip away.

"Everything's going to be fine, sweetie. Let's get you back to bed."

Mom puts her hand under my elbow to help me stand up, but I'm pasted to the floor, I can't move.

"Come on, Hattie. I'm right here. You'll be all right."

"What's going on? Why can't I see? Am I blind?"

"Don't you worry. We'll figure this out."

I skate my feet across the floor, too scared to take an actual step. "Am I sick? Will I get better?"

"Climb into bed."

I scramble onto the bed and Mom pulls up the covers and tucks me in. "I'm going to make a phone call. You hang on until I get back." I hear her take a sharp inhale. "Matt," she calls. "Come sit with your sister."

Matt plops down on the side of my bed. "I gotta hand it to you, Sis, you're a better actress than I thought. I have a new respect for you. Well done."

I try to stop crying as I listen to him, but I can't control myself. "I'm not joking. I can't see. How many times do I have to tell you?"

Matt chuckles. "Mom's gone. You can tell me the truth."

"This is the truth."

"Try blinking. Is there something in your eye?"

His hand touches my eye. "Lie still. Let me look."

I hear him flick on my bedside lamp, then he leaves my bedside and lifts the window shade. The shade flaps as he lets in the light. "Do you have a flashlight in here?"

He knows I do. I keep one beneath my bed so I can read at night without getting caught.

"Under the bed," I remind him.

I listen while he forages behind the dust ruffle. "Got it," he says.

He flashes the light in my eyes, not blinding, but I detect a shadow. An ounce of relief settles in my chest as he holds my right eye open.

"Do you see anything?" I ask.

"Not in that eye. I'll look in the other one."

I wait while he examines my eye, the comforting touch of his fingers warm on my face.

"I don't see anything."

"The light isn't bothering me, but I can see kind of a shadow, like maybe the outline of your head."

"You can see how I styled my hair, right? I'm hoping Sue likes my new do."

I giggle. I can't help myself. If I didn't know better, I'd say Matt was way older than me, the way he already loves girls so much. He got in big trouble last year, when he was only in the third grade, for running his "Percha's Dating Service" in class. He fancied himself a matchmaker, charging a nickel to be the go-between for boys and girls who liked each other. For a quarter, he'd set up a playground date behind the flagpole at recess. A quarter is pretty steep, if you ask me. And if both kids paid, he made fifty cents. He got in all kinds of trouble—a meeting with the principal, Sr. Mary Margaret, and then one with my parents too. In my mind, he'd come up with a great idea, but no one agreed with me. And just a few days ago he's thinking of trying the whole thing over again at St. Mary's. He's fearless. Or crazy.

"Sue. Is she new?"

"She's a babe. Kind of like Lulu."

"Blonde, I'm guessing."

"Yeah, and she looks like she's about fourteen."

"Is she a fourth grader?" I can't imagine a girl looking like a lady when she is only nine.

Mom clears her throat as she comes into my bedroom. "I've made a doctor's appointment for you, Hattie. Grandma's on her way over so I can take you. She'll stay with the boys."

Mom brushes my hair back from my forehead. Her hand is cool and soothing.

"Matt," she says. "Get ready for school. You and Rob need to start walking. I'll write you a quick note in case you're late."

I close my eyes. Being blind seems easier if I keep them shut. Makes not seeing less real.

Matt squeezes my shoulder and leans down close. "Be strong, Sis. I'll see you after school. I'm sure this is nothing serious. Maybe you have a bug."

"Maybe." I stop to think over his words. "I hope you're right."

"I'm always right, remember?"

He sounds like Crackers. She'd say the same thing. If Crackers were here right now, she'd make a game of this. "Think of this, Hattie, you're getting dressed in the dark. Can you get your clothes on right side out, arms in your sleeves, pants on backwards?" I laugh to myself just thinking about her.

"What's funny?" Mom asks.

"Thinking about Crackers."

"I'm glad you've found something good to think about," she says. "I know you're scared, Hattie, and so am I, but I can't think of anything you've done lately to cause this. Hopefully we're dealing with something minor. Do you have a headache?"

I stop for a minute. "A little one, but not like the ones I had before I got my new glasses. Maybe my prescription is wrong. The doctor might have made the lenses too strong, or maybe too weak."

Mom hesitates for a few seconds before answering. "Maybe," she says, wistfulness in her voice. "You're sure you're not faking in order to get out of going to St. Mary's?"

Her question stings. Like I'd fake this. I'm about to burst into flames, I'm so fighting mad. If I open my mouth, fire will come out for sure.

"I'm sorry, Hattie, but you were so against going to St. Mary's. I can't help but wonder."

Sometimes, when I'm this furious, I can do things I wouldn't do normally. "I can dress myself. How long before we go?"

"We have an hour. I bet you're hungry."

"A little."

"Call me when you finish dressing," she says. "I'll get John and Larry ready while you're doing that. Then, I'll help you downstairs to breakfast."

"I'll come down myself."

"I don't want you to fall, honey."

"I won't." I'd like to scream at her, but I don't.

She takes a sharp inhale. "Well, all right. But promise me you'll call me if you need anything. Anything at all."

"I will."

The door clicks shut as she leaves my room. I remember reading the book "Follow My Leader" last year when I was in fourth grade. This kid, Jimmy, was blinded in a firecracker accident. He got a cane and learned to read Braille, and even had a leader dog.

I've always wanted a dog.

CHAPTER SEVEN

D R. MULDER IS A NICE MAN, I GUESS, IF YOU NEED A doctor. Mostly I hate the doctor's. Every time I go, I have to get a shot of some kind, and I'm not fond of needles, if you get my drift. The place smells funky too, like Mercurochrome and alcohol. And because all I can see are fuzzy blobs, the nauseating scent is all I notice.

Mom guides me to a chair, and I sit like a statue while she checks in with the receptionist. She whispers, "Please, put us in a room as soon as possible."

When she sits down next to me, she pats my arm.

"Why do you want to go into a room? Are you embarrassed to be with me?"

"Of course not, Hattie. I'm just anxious for the doctor to see you."

My heart starts racing like a ball in the Mouse Trap game. "Are you scared? Do you think I'm really blind? Do you think they can fix me?"

"We'll find out," Mom says, all cheery, like I have tonsillitis or something simple. She's trying to make me feel better, I know, but this knot of dread tightens in my stomach.

"Hattie," the nurse announces.

Mom leans over and says, "That's you," like I can't hear now that I can't see.

I reach for her elbow since I remember how Jimmy held onto his friend's elbow in the book and let them guide him places. Mom's sleeve feels clammy, like she's sweaty.

"This way." She leads me into the exam room area where a nurse says, "Take a seat on the exam table, Hattie. The doctor will be in to see you shortly." Then, she murmurs under her breath, I guess to my mom, because she doesn't seem like she's talking to me. "Try not to worry."

This little pit of anger starts to burst in my chest. I'm the one who can't see, not Mom. Why are they talking to her and not to me?

I clench my fists and my jaw.

Mom leafs through a magazine.

"Did you call Dad?"

"Not yet. Let's see what the doctor has to say."

She's still acting all light and breezy, so I won't worry, but I see through that, even though my eyes aren't working. She's being like Dad was on the day the riots started—faking, trying to act calm.

I hate not being able to see, and say a silent prayer. *Please God, if you're listening, now's the time for a miracle.* If Jesus were still alive, I'd track him down and ask him to perform one for me. I don't mind being brave, but I have nothing to distract me, except fingering the button on my jacket and toying with the tassel from my hat. The soft wool strings skate through my fingers like silk.

What will I do if I'm blind? How will I go to school? I'm acting like a worrywart. I need to get over it. I have to start thinking more like Crackers.

I'll learn Braille, because I love to read. I won't need the flashlight anymore, and I'll be able to read in bed as late as I want. Cool. And I can come up with inventions to help myself and other blind kids. Yep. That's what I'll do.

The door creaks open and Dr. Mulder's heavy footsteps enter the room. "Hattie," he says in his booming voice. "Joan," he greets my mother. "Good to see you both. What's going on, Hattie?"

"I woke up this morning and everything was dark. I tried to rub my eyes and I put my glasses on and blinked for five whole minutes, but all I can see is gray. Like shadows and stuff. Dark splotches. Nothing clear. When my brother was sitting on my bed and shining a flashlight in my eyes, I sort of saw an outline of his head, but I might have been imagining it. Is it serious? Can you fix my eyes?"

"Let's have a look."

Dr. Mulder is always calm. He must have been trained to act unruffled no matter what the emergency. Like Grandma always says, "Act, don't react."

"I'm going to shine a light in your eyes, much stronger than the light your brother used. Let me know if you're uncomfortable at any point."

He cups my chin in his hand and says, "Open your eyes as wide as you can."

I stretch them open as far as I can. Dr. Mulder moves my head this way and that, but I don't notice a light at all. Not a good sign.

"Have you had a sudden bump on the head? Headaches?"

"I did break my glasses a few weeks ago when I fell off my bike," I say. "And I had lots of headaches until I got my glasses replaced last week. Since my new glasses, the headaches mostly went away. Do you think I need new glasses again?"

"I'm not sure, but I am interested in hearing about that fall. Did you hit your head when you fell?"

"Maybe. I'm not sure. Everything happened so fast."

Dr. Mulder addresses Mom. "Was she treated after the fall? I don't have a record of us seeing her. Did you take her to emergency?"

"No," Mom says, a tremor in her voice. "We watched her closely and a simple aspirin seemed to help when she complained of a headache."

"She may have had a concussion," the doctor says.

"Would that cause me to go blind?"

"Did you have any vomiting or feel nauseous after you fell?" he asks.

"I felt a little queasy right after. And then the headaches started. I guess the day after."

"Any sensitivity to light?"

"Come to think of it, yes, lights seemed bright to me. I squinted a lot, but I always do that, since I don't see very well without my glasses."

"There are several things that come to mind, but I can't be sure without further testing. I'm going to have you see a colleague of mine, an ophthalmologist. He's an eye expert, Hattie, and I'm hoping he can help us sort out what's going on with your eyes. Are you good in the dark?"

I straighten my shoulders. "Yes, as a matter of fact, I am. My brothers and I love to play tag after dark in the summer and

I'm good at finding my way around. I dressed myself this morning and combed my hair and brushed my teeth."

"Good for you," Doc Mulder says as he pats my shoulder. "Hold on a few minutes, will you? I'm going to call my friend right now. His name is Dr. Baker, and he has a daughter just your age. You'll like him. He's funny, and very smart."

"Will he be able to see her soon?" Mom asks, her voice still anxious.

"That's what I'm about to find out. Sit tight. I'll be right back."

After he closes the exam room door, I say to Mom, "Don't worry, I'm going to be all right. Dr. Baker will fix me up good as new." I'm not sure where I found the courage, but I lift my head, proud to be able to handle a crisis like this.

"Honey, I'm so proud of you," Mom says, her voice choking up.

A lump grows in my throat. *I will not cry. I will not cry.*

I swallow and twist my hands in my lap. "Do I need to stay up on this table?" I hate the rustling of the paper under my hips.

"I don't think so. Here, let me help you into a chair."

"No, Mom. I can do it myself."

She sits completely still while I ease myself down to the stepstool and remember where the chair is in the room. I reach out to feel in front of me and take small, careful steps, inching toward my memory. I find the seat, knees first, and turn to sit down.

Mission accomplished. If I'm not going to be able to see for a while, I better start figuring things out. If there's anything I hate, it's people helping me when I can do things for myself.

"How does my hair look? Be honest."

"Very nice, Hattie. You did a great job."

"Mom, if I'm going to be blind, you have to tell me the truth. You can't just say the right thing to make me feel better."

"So noted," Mom says, the first serious tone she's taken all day.

Doc Mulder waltzes back into the room, humming "Someone's in the Kitchen with Dinah." As Dad would say, "Must be a hazard of his profession," humming kids' songs 'cause he's a pediatrician.

"Good news," he says. "Dr. Baker will see you as soon as you can drive over to his office. Just tell the receptionist I sent you. They'll be waiting for you."

"Do you have any idea what's wrong?" Mom asks.

"Could be detached retinas."

I know the word retina, but only that the retina is part of my eye, not how it works. Detached means the retina is loose or something.

"What does the retina do?"

Dr. Mulder plants himself beside me and rests a hand on my knee. "You're a smart girl, Hattie. The retina helps turn the pictures in your eye into signals to your brain. You may have jarred something when you fell and some blood may have gotten inside your retina."

"Can they fix my eyes?"

"I'm going to be honest with you."

My heart catches in my ribs.

"Possibly, but we won't know without further tests. I'm not going to keep you any longer. You and your mother head over to Dr. Baker's right now. His office is near Grand River and Greenfield, Joan. Doris will give you the address and directions. Shouldn't take you longer than ten to fifteen minutes to drive over this time of day."

"Thank you, Doctor. I can't tell you how much we appreciate your help."

"My pleasure," Doc says. "You two be on your way."

Mom offers me her arm and leads me to the car. She waits for me to fumble with the handle and open the door for myself. I climb in the front seat and keep my eyes facing forward. I don't want to look like a blind girl. Don't want people to feel sorry for me. Plus, this won't last long. Dr. Baker will put my retinas back together pretty soon and I'll be good as new.

CHAPTER EIGHT

THE WINDSHIELD WIPERS FLAP BACK AND FORTH LIKE an angry bird. "Is it raining?"

"Just flurries, Ha...," Mom says. She's distracted. I can tell from the way her voice trails off when she says my name. "...I wish I could remember if Coyle is on this side of Greenfield or the other."

"The other side," I remind her. "Beverly doesn't live far from there."

My mind wanders to Beverly and Crackers. What are they doing right now? "What time is it?"

"Ten fifteen. Why?"

"Just thinking." My friends are in reading class. A pang hits my heart. I wonder if they know about me. No one would have told them, but their extrasensory perception should be on high alert—I hope they can tell something is happening to me by listening to their guts. My stomach tells me things like this all the time, like Matt's going to get in trouble again, or my heart will catch in my chest. I can feel when a bad thing is about to happen to Crackers or Beverly. Once, I knew right when the phone rang that Grandma was sick. I didn't have any hints either. The call came during dinner, not during the night when you expect bad news because the phone rings so late, but right as I was scooping some mashed potatoes into my mouth.

"Okay, I'll be right there," Dad said, before he hung up the phone and announced, "Genevieve has appendicitis. She's just been rushed to Mt. Carmel. I'll head over there right now."

"I want to go with you," Mom said. Grandma is Mom's mother after all. Dad has always assumed the role of savior in these situations, especially since Grandpa died. Something about it being the man's job to take care of emergencies. Not with us kids, but with the grown-ups. Adults are so weird.

"I'll handle this," Dad said. "I'll call as soon as I know something. You know how 'hurry up and wait' works."

Mom wrung her hands and wiped them on her apron, gathering the fabric in her fingers and twisting.

Dad kissed her forehead. "Don't worry about a thing. Kids, help your mother."

Even though I was only eight when this happened, I couldn't eat another bite.

I shut my eyes and squeeze them as tight as I can. I've tried sending messages to my friends like this before, and it can work. It really can.

Crackers and Beverly, if you can hear me now, I want you to know I'll be okay, but I really need to see the two of you, and soon. Come over after school today and visit. Please.

The car stops with a lurch. Mom must have hit the concrete barrier. She's rammed into the curb before when we've distracted her from driving. I'm guessing she's a bundle of nerves today, even though my brothers aren't here to bug her.

"We're here," she announces, like I don't know already.

I take her arm again and we walk across the parking lot. Snow falls harder now and the wind roars like a fierce grizzly. Giant flakes hit me in the face so hard they sting.

"This is the place," Mom announces, and I stand and wait so she can open the door. Nerves prickle up my arms and my tongue is tracing the back of my teeth over and over again.

She leads me inside and we don't even sit down, the receptionist waits right there to take me into a room. I figure it's not because I'm blind, because lots of the patients here must be blind. I almost feel like I fit right in, and my heartbeat slows.

"I'm Mary. Dr. Baker will be right in. He'll do some tests with you, Hattie, nothing to worry about though. Nothing painful, he'll just have you sit in front of a big machine so he can see into the back of your eye."

"Okay," I say.

Nerves still jump up my arms and twist in my stomach. Not two seconds later, the door creaks open.

"Hi there," a gravelly voice says. "I'm Doc Baker." I put my hand out and he shakes with me. His hands are big, sturdy and strong. Dad says you can tell a lot about a person from their handshake, like if they are solid and confident or wimpy and afraid. He says to shake hands as if you're self-assured and people will get the right idea about you. I grip Doc Baker's hand as hard as he grips mine, so he will think I'm not afraid. Even though I am.

"Mary said she told you what we will do today. Let me look in your eyes first though and tell me what happened when you took that fall."

I tell him the whole story. "My friends and I were riding

our bikes. My one friend, Beverly, was knocked off her bike by some kids who didn't like her skin color, and then they pushed me down too, because I'm friends with her. I think I landed on my face, because my glasses were broken in two and I had a gash over my eyebrow."

"Here?" he says as he touches the scar next to my left eye.

"Yes, right there."

I touch the spot when he moves his hand away, feeling the raised skin and remembering all over again how scary those minutes were when Maxine and her gang beat us up. Then I remember why I'm at the doctor's office.

"Can you fix my retina?"

"First I have to determine what the problem is."

I like how Dr. Baker uses big words with me and doesn't treat me like a kid.

He tells me he will flash a light in my eyes next, then do some tests. While he's using the light in my eyes, he keeps talking. "Have you had any double vision, blurry vision or difficulty focusing before this trouble today?"

"I squinted without my glasses as usual, but had some blurry vision too every now and then. No double vision though."

"Did you notice the blurriness increase when you went from sitting to standing, or changed positions all of a sudden?"

"No."

"Okay, then. Let's go visit the ophthalmoscope so I can see the back of your eye."

Mom's boots clack on the linoleum, and Dr. Baker asks her to wait for us. "I don't have much space in the room…"

"But…" Mom says before he has a chance to finish.

"If you aren't claustrophobic, you can sit on a stool in the corner."

This strikes me as the funniest thing I've ever heard and I have this picture of Mom sitting in the corner wearing a dunce hat. As soon as I can write again, I'll write a story about that. Crackers will love it.

We ramble down a long hall. The machine is gigantic from what Mom says, and I poise myself on a rolling stool. Mom ends up standing behind me, so I don't slide off the stool or away from the machine. She rests her hands on my shoulders and they keep me from shaking. Now, I'm scared. Not just a little bit either.

This must be what it feels like to wait in court when the judge is about to read your sentence. Time stops ticking and hangs over your head. A jail cell or freedom. A dark dingy cell with bars or bright sunshine and wide-open spaces. Those are the only choices. The same for me. I will either be able to see or I won't. It's not like Doc Baker can flip a switch and cure me, but I still wish he could. I wish he had a magic wand or something. I wish this was all a nightmare, and I'd wake up to an ordinary day at Crary, where the worst to happen is I get a bad grade on my math homework.

I steady my chin on a cup, made for the purpose of holding my head still, and the doctor tells me to look straight ahead. I'm already doing this, because I'm scared stiff. I know what it's like to sit without moving or breathing, whether I can see or not.

A few minutes pass by. "Mmm," Doc Baker says. I don't know what he means, but I detect a hint of worry in his voice, or am I imagining things?

"Okay," he says after another long minute. "Hattie, I'd like to have you wait in the exam room for a few minutes while I talk to your mother. Can you do that for me?"

"I think you should just tell me what you found. I'm ten

now. I should be able to hear what's going on with my eyes."

He must have exchanged a silent conversation with Mom, because seconds later, he says, "Let's go back to the room together then, and we'll talk."

Mom helps me down the hall. I can hardly make my legs work, knowing the news is dreadful. People are happy to give you good news right away. They always want to sit and "talk" when they are about to deliver the worst news possible.

We make our way back to the room. I perch on a cold hard chair, and Mom takes the seat next to me. Her hand feels clammy, not cool like it usually does if she touches my cheek or forehead when I'm sick.

Dr. Baker's footsteps stop and his stool squishes as he sits down.

He takes my hand. "We need to do surgery right away, Hattie. Your retinas are both detached. I can't tell you the outcome will be a good one. You've had quite a bit of bleeding going on, and I'm not sure how long the hemorrhages have been taking place. Mom can take you to Mt. Carmel Hospital right now, and they will admit you. I'll meet you there after the nurses prep you for surgery. This is our best chance of restoring your vision. Do you understand?"

I nod, my lips trembling. I can't utter a sound.

Mom asks, "May I use your phone, please?"

"Certainly," he says.

Mom leaves the room and I'm alone with the doctor, trying to be brave and fighting tears, but I can't hold them back, they just go running down my face like a leaky faucet.

"I'm one of the best doctors around, Hattie, and I promise to do my level best to help you see again."

I nod again, unable to speak.

"Have you ever had surgery before?"

I shake my head, tears streaming off my chin and onto my hands. Plop. Plop. Plop.

He gives me all kinds of details about what they'll do to me. I try to listen, I really do, but his words all jumble together—like I can't hear anymore either.

Mom steps back inside the room and Doc Baker rushes off to tell the nurse he has an emergency.

Me.

CHAPTER NINE

TIME VANISHES. I DON'T REMEMBER A SINGLE THING except smelling something sweet when the nurse put a mask over my nose and mouth. The next thing I know, I'm waking up in bed. For a few minutes, I don't know where I am, but then the day comes back to me in bits and pieces. I haven't been having a nightmare after all. This day is real.

I reach up to my face. Gauze wraps around my head like a turban pulled low to cover my eyes. Nothing hurts, but I still don't feel right, dizzy and nauseous and sick-scared.

"Hattie?" Mom's voice.

"Hi Mom."

"I'm here too," Dad says. "I'm proud of you. You're a brave girl."

"Just tell me what the doctor said. Did he fix my retinas? Was he able to stitch them back together?"

"We won't know for sure until the bandages come off. I'm sorry, Hattie, but you'll have to be patient." Dad's voice, deep with sadness.

"How long?"

"Just a few days." Mom pats my hand.

"A few days? I have to be like this for days? Just laying here wondering?"

"I'm afraid so," Dad says.

Mom's soft touch becomes a firm grip on my arm.

Friday morning. D-day, according to Doc Baker. He and my parents are gathered in my hospital room when he removes the bandages. He unwinds them slowly, and I feel like Tutankhamen, the mummy king. The seconds inch by, and when he loosens the last bit of gauze, I touch my eyes. For some reason, this makes me feel a little less anxious. I was worried they wouldn't still be there.

I make sure to open them, blink, and wait. Sometimes when I used to wake up in the morning, I had to open and close my eyes a few times before the world came into focus, so I'm telling myself to do the same thing, giving myself an extra chance.

"Hattie?" Dr. Baker says.

I hang my head to my chest. "It's no use," I say. "I can't see."

Tears well in my throat. I want to wake up in a different world, one where the sun shines like a beacon, and I can see brilliant rays sparkling on pool water. One where I can see the swift curls of my cursive on a sheet of paper. One where I can see Beverly Jo's huge brown eyes smiling at me and Crackers shoot hoops in the schoolyard. Never again will I see my friends' faces. I won't see Matt make horns behind my brothers' heads with his fingers, or my face in the mirror when I smile and make sure my teeth look glittery white.

"This was a difficult surgery, and sometimes the eye needs time to heal. We just have to wait and see I'm afraid. As for good news, you can go home. You'll feel better getting out of this place, being around your family and friends. Your school will provide you with rehabilitation services and teach you new ways to manage things. If your vision improves, as we all hope, then you'll have learned a few tricks to share with your friends."

"You mean I'll learn Braille and walk with a cane?" A knife slices through my heart as I ask the question, knowing the answer before I finish speaking.

"Yes, Hattie, you will." Dr. Baker delivers the news matter of fact. Dr. Mulder said he was funny. I haven't laughed since I met him. But he's right about one thing. I want to go home. Life will be easier there. I can live in my bedroom closet. I love to read in the little cubby I made in the corner, or maybe I can go to Grandma's house and live in her huge closet, the one with the fur coats and the cedar smell.

"I can't read." The words slip out before I realize I've said them aloud.

"The Library for the Blind has talking books. You can listen to books, and they are adding more titles all the time," Doc Baker says.

"I'll call them this afternoon, Hattie." Mom tries to reassure me, but I don't want anybody to talk to me right now. They're trying to make me feel better, but there's no fixing me right now. *Stop trying to make it right.*

The room goes silent. You could hear dust fly. After the longest minute on the planet, Dr. Baker clears his voice. "I'll get your discharge papers ready, Hattie, then you're free to go home."

"I'll speak to you in the hall," Dad says to the doctor. Their footsteps trail off and I'm left alone with Mom.

"Come on, let's get you dressed."

"I'm not a baby. I can do it myself."

"All right," she says. "I'll lay your clothes next to you on the bed. Would you like me to stay with you while you dress, or would you like some privacy?"

"Privacy," I say, snarly as a snake.

As soon as she leaves the room, I want her back, but I don't want to scream or shout to her, so I pull on my underwear, legs in the wrong holes, and have to start over again. Three attempts later, I figure out what leg needs to go where, then find the tags on my shirt and slacks. At least those itchy tags are useful for a change. My socks aren't a problem, but even when they go on easy, my heart is empty, just like my eyes.

I lie back on my pillow and close my eyes. Doesn't seem to matter if they are opened or closed anymore.

Mom knocks on the door and I let her in.

Two hours later I'm home, propped on the corner of the couch while Mom makes me some hot chocolate and Dad heads back to school. He's missed a ton of days since I've been blind, and he hustles back to take over fourth hour for his substitute. He has a midwinter concert coming up and has a lot of catching up to do.

Just like me. I can't even think about how far behind I am in school. Besides, I'm a St. Mary's student now. I never even made the first day after Christmas break. Who cares, I tell myself.

Mom asks me to come to the table, and Grandma says she

will help me. I realize how much I've missed Grandma. She couldn't visit me at the hospital because she was busy taking care of my brothers, but she told Mom she'd stay at our house until Saturday, three days from now, to help get me settled.

Her plumeria perfume wafts into the room before she even reaches me. The familiar scent reassures me, and for a millisecond I feel like everything will be all right.

"I made homemade macaroni and cheese for lunch," she says. "Your favorite."

I want to snipe at her. Everybody is being so nice, but instead of making me feel better, they're just making me mad. If I weren't blind, they wouldn't treat me like this.

"Thanks," I say as I stand up and wait for her to offer me her arm.

We slog our way to the kitchen and I only bump into the wall once. Grandma is careful to give me specific instructions and when I sit down, she takes my hands and places the tips of my fingers on the plate.

"Macaroni and cheese at ten o'clock. Carrot sticks at six o'clock."

Thinking about my plate like a clock helps me find my food without fumbling around. I try using a fork on my macaroni, but I'm embarrassed to miss my mouth and stab myself, or drop food all over, so I use my spoon instead.

I manage okay, and neither Mom nor Grandma has much to say about whether or not I'm making a mess. I'm glad John and Larry are down for their naps and Matt and Rob are at school. At least they won't see me make a fool of myself.

I huddle on the couch in the den after lunch. Mom turns on the television and I listen to Milky the Clown, seeing him in my mind's eye and even laughing at a joke or two. Voices in the kitchen keep distracting me, so I turn down the set and listen as hard as I can.

Mom clears her throat, and I think she's about to tell Grandma what's she making for dinner, but instead she says, "Did you know Stevie Wonder goes to a special school?"

I bite my tongue the shock hits me so fast. *Is she thinking of sending me there?*

"He's a prodigy," Grandma says, missing mom's point. Mom isn't thinking he goes to a special school because he's a talented musician, but because he's blind.

"Michigan School for the Blind. They teach kids how to navigate the world when they are struggling with sight problems."

"Wait a minute. Are you saying you're thinking Hattie should go there?"

"It's a residential school, she would learn very quickly, considering how smart she is, and we could have her come home some weekends."

I crawl through the hallway, planting myself outside the kitchen doorway, knees folded into my chest and barely breathing. I'm dumbfounded. Frozen in time, but the anger that rises from my belly swells like a bursting bruise, and words pound inside my brain. *I will not be sent away. I can't believe you would even consider shipping me off. This is just another example of prejudice and bigotry. Just because I'm blind, doesn't mean I have to be put away. You're treating me like I'm not a real person anymore just because I lost my sight. Big deal, Stevie Wonder is there. I don't care. I'm not going.*

I hear Grandma's chair scrape back from the table and her footsteps trail over to the sink.

"Calm down for a minute and listen, Mother."

Grandma turns on the faucet and I can barely hear.

"You want…best for…Hattie…decide."

Turn off the water. This is my future you're talking about.

"Visually Impaired students…Lincoln Park…could drive her…Braille…use a cane…"

I weigh this option. Lincoln Park isn't that far away, but still, I'll be away from Crackers and Beverly. And besides… What about St. Mary's? I thought I was signed up to go there.

I stand up and bump my knee into the wall, but I could care less, I just stomp upstairs.

After hitting the stair rail and nearly missing the last step and falling down to the landing, I make it to my room, slam the door and fall into bed. I can't believe Mom doesn't come after me. I shut my eyes and pull the covers over my head.

I wake up not having a clue how long I slept, but voices chatter in the hall outside my room. A tap on the door comes next, and the door bursts open.

"Hey, Chickadee," Crackers says.

Beverly's soft voice follows. "Hattie."

Even though I can't see, my world brightens. A smile covers my face and I scoot to the side of my bed, lean forward, and stretch my arms out to them. They wrap me in a giant hug, and I want to stay in the moment forever.

"I'm so glad you're here."

"What's the word, Hattie Bird?" Crackers asks.

I give them all the details I can think of, even how I peed on the floor when I missed the toilet and how I had to wash my legs and throw my gown in the wastebasket before anyone found out what happened. Crackers thought peeing on myself was the funniest thing she ever heard. Beverly patted my shoulder, offering me her mortified sympathy.

"Are you going to get a cane?" Crackers asks. No surprise she's full of questions.

"Yep."

"Think of the fun we'll have. Will you let me pretend I'm blind? I want to wear a blindfold so I can see what it's like."

"I'll help you get around school," Beverly offers.

"Mom wants to send me away to a special school for blind kids. Either in Lansing or Lincoln Park. She wants to get rid of me now that I'm blind."

Crackers slaps me on the back. "Bet your bottom dollar, you're not going to those schools."

"What do you mean?"

Beverly shushes Crackers. "I don't know if we're supposed to tell her."

Crackers shoves Beverly into me and we both tumble back onto the bed.

My pulse quickens. "Tell me what? What do you know that I don't?"

"You're coming back to Crary. St. Mary's doesn't want you because you're…um…"

"Blind. You can just say it. I wouldn't expect anything less from you guys. You're my best friends. My honest friends."

"Fine. You're blind," Crackers says with a flourish.

"Mom practically stutters when she talks about my eyes, and Dad isn't much better, pussyfooting around—'the trouble with your eyes, the blurriness you're experiencing'—it's all hogwash. And I overheard the whole thing. She's sending me away, I told you."

"Stop being melodramatic and listen. I'm trying to tell you.

This the best news ever." Crackers can't control herself, she hugs me so tight I might snap in two.

"Wait. I get to come to Crary?" Is this a silver lining? I know enough to look for the bright spot, to be ever hopeful. Going to Crary is my dream come true. Maybe God works in mysterious ways. And maybe my vision will be back before I pass fifth grade. The more I think about it, the more my heart sinks. They're mistaken. There's nothing for blind kids at Crary.

"This is going to be so cool, Hattie. Will you learn to read Braille? You can teach Bev Jo and me and we can have a secret language, make up codes. Maybe you'll even get one of those cool guide dogs. Get a girl dog and I'll put bows on her ears. They are way better than boy dogs. They don't lift their legs to pee and they don't hump everything in sight."

Beverly laughs, not her sweet little tee-hee giggle, but a hearty belly laugh. Speaking of peeing, she might wet her pants right now. I wish I could see her, but in my mind's eye I do, her eyes are shimmering from the tears forming at the edges. I just know they are. She always cries when she laughs so hard.

I reach out and touch her hair, to be sure it feels the way I remember, coarse and frizzy, and she runs her fingers through mine.

"Hold on a second. How do you know I'll be going to Crary?" I scratch my head. How do Crackers and Beverly know and I don't?

"We overheard your Mom on the phone when we were waiting in the back hall. Your Grandma had to check and make sure we could come up and see you," Crackers boasts.

I tip my head toward Beverly. "It's true, Hattie. Your mom told your grandma that Sr. Maxine said they don't have anyone to teach you how to be blind at the Catholic school." It hits me then. The principal at St. Mary's is named Maxine, and so is my enemy at school. This can't be a coincidence.

I plop down on my bed. "What do you know about Crary? Mom said Lincoln Park, not Crary." My stomach twists into a giant pretzel. Is this God's way of letting me know my wish was both good and bad? Is this what divine intervention means? If so, I might not be blind forever. God must have made me blind in order to teach me a valuable lesson.

"Here's what I heard." Crackers leans close and whispers like she'll be in a ton of trouble if anyone finds out she was eavesdropping. "Since your Dad teaches in Detroit and has a blind student in the band, he's arranging for one of the teachers in Lincoln Park to come to your school to help you before school and on their lunch hour. You are so lucky! We all are!"

My brain goes into slow motion or something, because it takes me a while to work all this out in my head, and to convince myself it's okay to believe what Crackers just told me.

"Hattie," Beverly says, "are you okay?"

"Sort of," I answer. "I was just wondering about God and if he made me blind so I could stay with you."

Crackers makes a "tsk, tsk, tsk" sound. "Hattie, you've got this religion thing all wrong. That's why I don't want to go to church. Your mind starts confusing things. God didn't have anything to do with making you blind, those kids who knocked you down did. I'm about ready to bash in some heads."

"You'd just get in a heap of trouble, and what good would that do? Besides, they didn't mean to make me blind."

Beverly rests her spindly fingers on my arm. "Aren't you mad, Hattie?"

"You forgave Mrs. Simmons for saying nasty things about you and calling you the "N" word. I can forgive Maxine and

Darryl and Timmy and Joe. They meant to hurt me, but they didn't think I'd wind up blind." *Secretly, I'd like to wallop those kids, but I want to at least try to be as forgiving as Beverly. Saying it out loud sounds like a lie though. A lie I hope to live up to.*

Beverly pats my arm. "I'm proud of you, Hattie. Only the most courageous people can be forgiving. You know Crackers and I will do whatever we can to help you, and I'm sure you'll be able to see again soon, once your eyes heal more. Mom and I are praying day and night."

Beverly's mom, Mrs. Nichols, is one of the sweetest ladies I know. Beverly inherited her kind heart. She's so lucky.

Crackers pipes up. "When will you get a cane? Wait, isn't there a cane in the basement? I thought I saw one when we spent the night."

"You probably mean the walking stick my dad found when we were hiking at Rouge Park one Saturday. A cane for a blind person is different—white with a red band on the bottom, so people will know I'm blind."

"I have a far out idea. Why don't you pretend you can see? Try right now. Just sit on your bed and Bev Jo and I will stand in different parts of your room. Listen to us talk, then walk toward our voices. We'll make sure the path is clear." She instructs Beverly to stand by the door to my balcony, and I hear furniture scape across the floor as she clears a path and then bolts to the other side of the room.

Beverly starts to talk. "Stand up, Hattie, and walk toward my voice. Your bed is on the right, so stay in a straight line for about five steps, then turn right for about three." I follow her directions and voice, and make my way to her without bumping my knee or planting my face on the floor. She wraps me in a hug when I stand in front of her without knocking her over.

Crackers snaps her fingers on the far side of the room. She means this like clapping, and I groan. I'm not a dog. A vision of my bedroom sparks in my mind's eye. I know where everything is, my desk, the old painted maple chair, my bookcase, even the stash of candy in the bottom dresser drawer. My friends are right. This is the perfect place for me to pretend I can see.

CHAPTER TEN

I DON'T WANT BEVERLY AND CRACKERS TO LEAVE, BUT I'M dying to find out if what they told me is true. If I can still be a Crary student with my friends, I can put up with being blind for a few weeks.

After Crackers and Beverly leave, Grandma hums. I follow her song into the kitchen, taking tentative steps. I hate taking baby steps, but the more I practice walking, the more sure-footed I'll become.

"What's for dinner? Smells like chicken, potatoes and carrots in here."

"You have a keen nose, Hattie. Add cherry Jello for desert and you have the complete menu."

"Is it true St. Mary's doesn't want me? Beverly and Crackers said they overheard Mom on the phone with Sr. Maxine."

"Mom and Dad will talk to you about school. It's not my place."

"Please, Grandma, please," I plead as I bang my knee into

a chair.

"Hattie, be careful." Her voice goes all shaky and sad. "I'm so sorry about your eyes."

She sits down next to me and pulls me onto her lap. I rest my head on her shoulder and inhale her sweet scent. Her silky curls brush my cheek. "I'm so, so sorry."

"Don't worry. I'll be good as new before long. Beverly says my eyes need more time to heal is all, and if I can go to Crary, she and Crackers will help with anything I need. Crackers is making a game of my blindness. I'll be okay. Like you always tell me, 'Look for the silver lining.' Being with my friends is the best possible thing that could happen to me."

She starts crying harder then, and for some reason, I feel sad too, and tears start to flow.

Crying is contagious. Worse than the flu.

Pretty soon Mom strolls into the kitchen. Once she sees us, she wraps her arms around us, and she's bawling. Dad walks in a few seconds later. "What's this?" he says. And before I know it, our faces touch in a giant hug and we are an overflowing puddle of tears. All of us.

Here comes Matt. "What the...?" A second later his arms fold around our group hug.

"Who's hungry?" Dad asks, the great equalizing force. Dad's sensitive enough, but uncomfortable when there are lots of tears and no quick fix. In his mind, food fixes everything.

"Why else would I be here?" Matt says.

I laugh, from some normal place, and realize I'm starving, and my tears were a reaction to everyone else's sadness, not mine. I'd rather get on with being blind than wallow in pity. "Matt is all about the food," I tease. "Want me to set the table?"

"Great idea," Matt says, "but my job is setting the table.

You missed out on jobs when you were in the hospital. Nice going! You're washing dishes this week. Do you think you can clean them if you can't see?"

Mom takes a sharp inhale. "Matthew! Be nice."

"I'm just asking."

"We'll all pitch in on Hattie's jobs until she learns how to do things."

"There are a lot of things I can still do. Don't treat me like a baby. If Rob dries the dishes, he can let me know if I miss a spot, like usual."

It's settled. Matt sets the table and we gather for dinner—Grandma squeezes in between the high chair and me. She cuts Larry's chicken into bits, my standard job, and offers to cut up my chicken too. I let her. While I'm ready to try almost anything, the idea of using a knife is intimidating. Having one body part "out of service" is quite enough.

After dinner, Dad suggests a game of Crazy Eights. I guess this blindness thing will take a while for all of us to get used to. Life is still the same, but different too.

I wash the dishes, plunging my hands into the dishwater and scrubbing the plates cleaner than I would have when I could see, and only clanging a few plates on the faucet as I rinse them. Rob is sweet—he takes the clean dishes right from my hand, and tells me when I'm about to put something in the wrong place.

Later on, I put my nightgown on backwards, but figure that out too. The saddest I am all day is when I remember I can't read at night. Or any other time, for that matter.

At bedtime, Mom and Dad come to tuck me in. They both

sit on the side of my bed. Mom right next to me. Dad behind her.

"We have some news."

My stomach starts to jiggle. I say a quick prayer. This could be the news about Crary, but then I remember how I was sure they would let me stay with my friends before, and none of those wishes had worked out.

"St. Mary's doesn't have a teacher who specializes in training students with visual…um…impairments. Crary does. They can send in a special teacher to work with you, to tutor you in Braille and supply you with other techniques to help you learn. A mobility specialist can also come to Crary and show you how to walk around school, use a cane, and teach your friends how to guide you to class, the cafeteria, and the gym," Dad says.

I picture Crackers leading me into the janitor's closet and leaving me there, smelling the ammonia and Pine Sol they use to clean.

"This won't be easy, Hattie," Mom says.

I'm determined to prove them wrong, but my arms tingle and a lump clogs my throat. I've pretended this is a fun game to play, being blind, but way down deep, I know better. If I'm blind forever, my life will stink.

I sink back on my pillow and bite my lip. Who will be with me? And will Mrs. Simmons be fake nice to me, but make fun of me behind my back like she did to Beverly for being black? If Maxine and Joe and Timmy pick on me, will I be strong enough to stand up to them? Is prejudice contagious? If you're prejudice about one thing, does it spread like a rash? Are you prejudice about everything?

"Could the teacher come to the house for a few weeks so when I go back to school, I already know how to do things? If

I bump into walls, and can't write, I'll be embarrassed. I don't think I can do this."

Snot clogs my throat. If I could hide until I know how to be blind, I'd rather do that.

"I know it's scary, honey," Mom says, "but your teacher called when you were getting ready for bed. Her name is Miss Tyler, and she's the one who will be helping you in class. The mobility specialist is Mrs. Abernathy, and she will meet you at school first thing in the morning. She's going to give you tips on making your way around school. Everything is in place, now don't you worry."

"I don't want to go. How about I stay home and you teach me?"

"You're tired. This was a long day, your first day home. Lots of excitement and lots of nerves. You can do this, Hattie. I have confidence in you. So does your father."

I don't want to let Dad down. He has more faith in me right now than I do in myself, but can't he let me off the hook for once? If only I was still nine, or the youngest kid in our family and not the oldest.

"Get some rest," Mom says. "The world will look brighter in the morning."

Maybe so. Maybe when I wake up in the morning, I'll be able to see.

CHAPTER ELEVEN

WHEN I WAKE UP, THE WORLD IS STILL A THICK thundercloud, and Mom's breathing heavy at the side of my bed. She has clothes picked out for me, and leaves me to get dressed. I inch to the bedroom door and listen to Matt and Rob in the bathroom, arguing about the Detroit Lions.

"Landry is way better than Munson. He's quicker on his feet, and his stats are way better."

"If Munson gets traded, I'm not watching another game."

Football. Who cares? I poke my head into the bathroom.

"Hey, Hattie, do you need some help?" Rob asks.

"I want to stay home."

"Who doesn't? At least you don't have to walk that far to school. We have a whole mile to go, and Mom says to bundle up. Only fifteen degrees out there."

"How am I going to walk to school? I can't see."

"We're going to drop you off on our way. Remember, the

special teacher comes early to meet you." Rob tries to be nice, but I don't even care.

"C'mon, Hattie," Matt says. "Let's get breakfast. Mom bought Trix."

Trix is my favorite cereal, and I'm hungry, so I let him talk me through walking to the stairs, then hold the rail so I can make my way down without falling.

"Can you give something to Beverly for me?"

"What?"

"Can you give something to Beverly for me?" he repeats.

"I heard you, but what on earth would you have for Beverly? You never even talked to her."

"Sure, I have," he says, all sheepish like.

"When?"

"When she and Crackers were here spending the night. I saw her yesterday when she was here too. She lives near St. Mary's, you know."

What the heck is he talking about? Sure, Beverly lives near St. Mary's, but why would he care?

"I'll slip the note in your school bag, but I want you to feel the paper, so you know the size and can remember what it is when you see her. Don't forget, okay?"

"I won't. What are you sending her?"

"None of your beeswax."

"She's my friend, Matt, you have to tell me."

"I could tell you, but how would you know I'm being honest if you can't see?"

"You're mean. I can ask her, that's how. She would never lie to me. You don't have to tell her to take care of me, or give her any tips or advice. I'll be fine without your help."

"Geez, Hattie, don't start thinking everything is about you."

"I don't! But why else would you be sending a note to Beverly? Do you have one for Crackers too?"

"Tomorrow I'll send one to her."

Mom's cheery when we reach the kitchen. "I've poured your cereal, Hattie. No milk, just as you like. And I strained your orange juice. No pulp."

We sit down and scarf breakfast, then hurry out the door. I show Matt how to let me hold his arm and lead me. He's still rattling on about how I better not forget to give Beverly the note. Rob runs ahead of us and makes snowballs and tries to hit us. He's sliding on the sidewalk though and lucky for us, he's not a great aim.

By the time we get to Crary, I'm anxious to see Crackers and Beverly. At the door, a lady greets us. "You must be Hattie."

"Yes, I am."

She says to Matt and Rob, "I've got her now, boys. Thanks for dropping her off."

Matt slaps me on the shoulder. "Have a good day, Sis." Rob gives me a quick hug and they're off.

"I'm Miss Tyler, Hattie. Come on inside. It's bitter cold out here today."

She sounds like a teenager, but helps me inside and tells me a few things as she leads me down the hall to a little room next to the office. The room smells musty—I'm guessing I'm the only one Miss Tyler sees at the school. I haven't seen any other blind students at Crary.

She keeps talking. "I had you come early today so we could try out a cane. Your mom told me how tall you are, so this one should work fine. Take off your coat and set it on the chair to your left."

Stuffing my hat and gloves into my sleeve, I reach out with

the back of my hand, guiding my coat toward the chair.

"Your other left," Miss Tyler says.

Mission accomplished, until I hear the heap slide onto the floor. I'm determined to do this, so I reach down to grab my jacket. Whack! I smash my forehead on the arm of the chair. Why does one simple task have to be so difficult?

"Don't worry," Miss Tyler says. "You'll take a few lumps, but soon you'll have all this mastered."

"I can't even put my coat on a chair without banging my head."

"You've never bonked your head before? You've never dropped your coat?"

She has a point.

"I'm ready," I say after managing to stuff my belongings on the chair.

"Here, take the cane."

Miss Tyler leads me into the hall and positions the cane so I hold it in the center of my body pointing down at a 45-degree angle. She says to swing the cane in an arc.

"This stick will become your dance partner. If you use the cane properly, you won't step on your partner's toes."

I like how she jokes and sounds like a writer. I like to think about things in the same way. Metaphors. "Can you teach me to read and write?"

Her laughter echoes in the hall. "I'm going to teach you all those things, Hattie, and Mrs. Abernathy will be your mobility instructor, but she had another appointment this morning, so you'll have me today."

"I want you to be my teacher for everything."

"Mrs. Abernathy is the mobility expert," she says. "You'll like her. I promise."

She grips my hand and swings the cane with me, so I can feel the motion.

"Now, tap the cane to the right as you take a step forward with your left foot. This way, you know your path is clear when you walk."

I try, but I can't seem to walk in sync.

"We all struggle when we dance with a new partner, Hattie. Just keep practicing. You'll get the hang of this soon enough."

Dad says with practice, I can do whatever I set my mind to do.

I think, "tap left, step right, tap right, step left," over and over in my head as I go up and down the hall.

"I'm walking, I'm walking!" I shout, right before I collide headfirst into a locker. The loud metal clunk is better than the thud of a cement wall, I suppose. I rub my hand over the goose egg on my forehead and wince. Now I have two lumps instead of one. After today, my noggin should be used to this, or maybe I should borrow Matt's football helmet. Crackers would say, "Nice look." I know she would. Maybe I should get bangs to cover the bruises.

"You got ahead of yourself. When you tap the cane and feel resistance, then you know there's a barrier.

"Back up and try again. When you feel the cane bump up against something, reach out with the back of your left hand, turn, and tap the object. You can try any of those techniques to help yourself."

Once I practice a bit longer, we go over to the stairs. Since my classroom is on the second floor, I have to learn how to go upstairs. And fast. School will be starting soon, and I want to be able to negotiate the stairs before my classmates arrive for the day.

"There are two ways to do this," Miss Tyler says. "If there is a handrail, use that. If not, place your cane on the first step then tap forward. This will let you know how wide the step is and how many steps you will need to take to the next step. Don't count the stairs, because different staircases have different steps. Rely on your cane if there isn't a handrail, but always use the rail if you find one."

I reach to my right, remembering the stair rail. Mrs. Simmons told Crackers there was no riding on the rail. "This isn't a slide, Miss McCracken," she said one day when Crackers had a glint in her eye. Mrs. Simmons knew just what she had in mind.

Making my way up the steps is easy once I think about that.

"Now, find your locker."

The idea of locating my locker is like searching out a four-leaf clover. Mine is the fifth from the end row, but how will I find it without being able to see? I put my left arm across my chest and reach out the back of my right hand, to feel my way, and count. Once I reach my locker, I ask Miss Tyler, "Is this mine?"

My tummy twists. I won't be able to work the combination.

"Yes," she says. "Now reach for the handle."

I do what she asks, but can't imagine how I will open it. "What…"

As my fingers trail down the face of my locker, I find something new. A smile grows across my face.

"We put a key lock on your locker!" Miss Tyler says. "Here you go."

I stretch out my hand and she places a key inside. Now, I have to figure out how to insert the key without seeing the way it fits into the lock, but after only three tries, the lock falls open.

This part is easy! I open my locker and put away my lunch and school bag.

With a start, I remember Matt's note for Beverly, and tuck the slip of paper in my skirt pocket. I consider asking Miss Tyler to read it to me, but then think better. I'll have Crackers read the message, and then I'll decide if I want to pass the note to Beverly or tell him I forgot. If he's telling Beverly to watch out for me, I won't bother giving the note to her.

Miss Tyler helps me inside the classroom to my desk. "How will I read and write during class?"

"We've ordered Braille textbooks for you, but learning Braille will take a while. Later today, we will have our first session. Mrs. Simmons suggested you leave during reading class today, and you and I will work together then."

"How will my fingers be able to read dots on a page?" I know Helen Keller learned Braille, but she was a genius.

"You'll be surprised what you can do, Hattie. Braille is really quite simple. There are only six dots to learn, each combination of the dots stands for something different, like letters or numbers, then specific combinations serve as shortcuts for words."

"Like a code."

"Precisely."

My mind shifts to sharing codes with Crackers and Beverly. This might be fun.

"How fast can I learn? I don't want to miss out on my studies. Once I get behind, it's impossible to catch up."

"The more you practice, the faster you'll learn."

I can't wait to get started.

CHAPTER TWELVE

SOON THE ROOM FILLS. MRS. SIMMONS ARRIVES FIRST, and offers to change my seat to the front of the room. Before Christmas break, Beverly and Crackers sat next to each other and I sat next to my nemesis, archrival Maxine. The thought of having to sit by her now makes my heart sink.

"Could I possibly sit near Crackers or Beverly?"

Thankfully, she says, "Yes."

What a relief. I can't handle Maxine's snotty voice or her smart aleck comments. Mrs. Simmons ends up moving Beverly next to me.

Beverly lays her hand on my shoulder as I sit at my desk, afraid to move. What will the kids think of me now that I'm blind? Will they still tease me like they used to? Timmy and Joe called me "four eyes" all the time when I wore glasses. Will they call me "no eyes" now? I bite my lip.

"You're going to be great, Hattie. Don't be scared."

Beverly knows me better than anyone. If only I could see

her big brown eyes.

"Hattie! You're here!" Crackers stands smack in front of me, tapping out a happy little rhythm on my desktop.

"Can I go home now?"

"Stop talking nonsense. We're going to have the best day. Hey, is this your cane? Can I try it? Can we go in the hall and try out Hattie's cane, Mrs. Simmons?"

"Miss McCracken, take your seat. Only a minute until the late bell and we have a lot of work to do today."

Crackers groans. "Spoil sport!" she says, before whispering to me, "At recess, you can show me how to be blind."

I pray for the morning to zoom by. Recess will be the best part of my day, for sure.

Beverly pats my hand. "There's no reason to be nervous. I'll help you with everything. I even came up with a cool idea. If you use a ruler, you can still write on paper. Press down hard with your pencil—don't use a pen—too hard to make indentions on the page. I practiced last night by closing my eyes. You'll see."

"Far out!" I reach inside my desk and pull out some loose leaf paper, a pencil, and my ruler. I line up the page so the holes are on the left, and then place the ruler on the paper, lining it up as straight as I can with the edges of the paper. "Is it straight?" I ask.

"Perfect," Beverly says. I trust her to tell me the truth.

I write my name from memory, pressing hard like Beverly told me so I can feel what I write after I finish. The hard part will be making spaces between my words. I jump my pencil over a tad after I write "Hattie" and stop after I write "Percha," my last name. "How does my cursive look? Did I write straight? Are the names separate?"

"Looks spiffy. See, you can do anything if you try."

Mrs. Simmons begins class, and I begin my first day of school as a blind kid. So far, so good.

Math, my worst subject when I could see, is even more wicked without eyes. I need to do everything on paper, but without being able to line up my numbers and not seeing the board, I feel like I'm in a classroom where Mrs. Simmons speaks German instead of English.

Joey, who sits on the other side of me, leans over. His hot breath coils around my neck. "Why aren't you writing anything down?" He's teasing me. Being cruel, as usual. I choose to ignore him, but a blistering blush rises up my neck, and my face begins to burn.

Creep. Meanie.

I bite my lip and turn to Beverly. "This is impossible."

"Don't worry. You have to be patient."

I start to giggle. Me, patient?

"Shhh," Beverly says.

There's a commotion behind me, then Mrs. Simmons' voice. "Miss McCracken, what is it?"

"When I flipped the fractions to make the reciprocal, number two fell off number three and cartwheeled over the multiplier and somersaulted onto the divisor! Can you dig it?"

Crackers, just being her usual class clown self.

Why she has to try Mrs. Simmons' tolerance now, I have no idea.

Mrs. Simmons says, "Let's take a break and go outside for recess. Bundle up."

Nerves jitter through my body. I'm not ready for any of

this. I'm not even sure how to stand up and move through the room. "Need help, Hattie?" Beverly's sweet strains soothe me.

I let out all of my breath. "What would I do without you?" *I'm in over my head. I can't imagine how to go outside. Maybe if I ask Mrs. Simmons, she will let me stay indoors. Not like there is anything for me to do in here. I can't read. I guess I could write, since Beverly taught me how.*

"Hattie, Hattie, blind as a Battie," Crackers says. "You can practice your radar. What a gas!"

Crackers gives me confidence, and I remember what Dad always says. "Stay positive and poised, and people will treat you like you know what you're doing. Never act like a target. People take advantage of victims."

He's right. I can't be a victim, even though the first thing I think to do is hide. I've always liked hiding inside myself, away from uncomfortable situations, but now isn't the time. If I'm going to be blind, I have to face the facts, and make myself do the things I least want to. Even when I don't feel up to it, even when I feel weak and scared.

"Hattie," Mrs. Simmons says, "you go first. Miss McCracken, please help your friend to her locker and assist her in whatever way you can. The rest of class will wait until you and Hattie are down the stairs.

"Class, your homework for tonight is…"

Crackers stands by my side. "C'mon, Hattie. Let's go. This is far out! We get to leave first!"

I want Beverly to come too. She's steadier than Crackers. More reliable. And trustworthy. But when Crackers takes my hand and pulls me out of my seat, I take her arm and let her guide me out to the hall.

"Wait! I need my cane. Miss Tyler showed me how to go

down the hall this morning."

"Got it right here, Sugar Plum. You can show me how to use it too. I want to come over after school and you can blindfold me so I can see what it's like to be blind. I can't wait."

"Being blind might be fun for a few minutes, but not being able to see is no picnic, I warn you."

"You have a bad attitude. You can't smell the roses if you forget to sniff. You're like a super spy now, Hattie. You can hear things the rest of us can't, know things because you're sensing things the rest of us ignore because we're busy checking things out."

"You aren't making one ounce of sense right now," I snarl. "Not one single iota of sense."

"Like I don't know how hard life is," she snaps back. "Go ahead, sob, sob, sob, Hattie. I'll listen to you, but I won't feel sorry for you.

This is for your own good. We're still the Dream Girls, and we're tough."

Sweat beads on my forehead. Putting on my coat, boots, hat, and gloves, plus making my way downstairs and outside is more than I can fathom. By the time I reach the doors, I'll be ready to scream.

Crackers must see the perspiration dripping off my forehead, because she swipes her hand across my face. "Never let 'em see you sweat."

"Is that a sports saying or something?"

"Sure."

"Okay." She has me at my locker now and I give her the key. She hands it back to me and gives me an order, "Open your locker."

I do what she says. She's right. I'm having a pity party. She doesn't want to come.

"Fine," I retort, and she slaps me on the back and knocks me off balance. She titters, and I join in. Pretty soon, we're both laughing like hyenas.

Mrs. Simmons chastises us from the classroom doorway, "No dawdling, girls," like we are up to no good, which we are, and like we're normal kids goofing off, which we are.

For some reason, this gives me just the boost of confidence I need. I'm normal. I haven't thought of myself as normal for at least a week, I guess, maybe two. I lost all track of time, lately, but this feels good. Crackers pokes me with my cane as I'm trying to pull my wool cap down over my ears. I grip my boot and flop down on the floor to put it on. These boots are the worst—they grab onto my shoes and won't let go.

"That one goes on your other foot," Crackers says.

"I do this wrong even when I can see."

This sets us into another giggling fit, and I shush Crackers. "We're going to get in trouble again."

"When has that ever stopped me?"

CHAPTER THIRTEEN

I'M ABOUT TO CLOSE MY LOCKER WHEN I REMEMBER THE note. I lift up my jacket and pull the slip of paper from my pocket. "Before we go outside, I need you to read this. My brother wrote a note to Beverly. If he's telling her to take care of me, I'm tossing this in the trash. He's probably looking out for me, but I can do this myself."

I hold the handrail when we go down the steps, and Crackers starts making soft whooping sounds under her breath.

"What?"

"This is big dust, Hattie."

"Well, tell me. Don't keep me in the dark."

"In the dark. That's funny, Hattie. Hilarious, in fact." She elbows me in the ribs and almost knocks me down the stairs.

"Oops, sorry. I forgot you couldn't see."

"That's cool. What does the note say?"

"He wants to go steady!"

"What the heck?" I whisper, then when the words sink in,

I moan. "Ewww. That's totally gross."

"I saw them talking when we were at your house for the sleepover. Beverly was batting her big baby browns at him. You know how she wants a white boyfriend."

"Why Matt? He's too young for her. Can you imagine if anyone finds out?"

"Are you grossed out because she's black and your brother is white?"

"Of course not. That has nothing to do with it."

"Then you're just opposed to them swapping spit."

"Now you're making me barf."

"You've never been in love?"

"Of course not. Have you?"

"Boys. Schmoys. But Beverly is way ahead of us in that department. She's her own person. If she's ready for love, you're not going to stop her."

"I would never stop her. I'm just thinking."

"Thinking is dangerous, Hattie, and if there's a sin you're guilty of, it's thinking too hard and too much."

Not like this is the first time Crackers has told me this. You would think by now I would have learned this lesson. Must be my personality to overthink. I'm a worrier. There's no way to stop. "You can't tell Beverly I let you read this."

"My lips are sealed." She makes a zipping sound.

"Thanks."

"For what?"

"For being my friend even though I'm blind, and for making extra noise so I know what's going on. Even though I can't see you, I can still see you, you know?"

"I get your drift," Crackers says as she squeezes my arm.

I realize I've made it all the way to the back door using my cane. I didn't crash or stumble or fall on my nose.

"I'll give the note to her when we're doing handclaps."

Crackers itches to play football with the boys. I can tell because her voice trails off in the other direction. She's eyeing them, I bet. Hoping they won't start without her. Like that would ever happen. "You have to let me know what she says. Promise?"

"I've already told you this much. Maybe Beverly will want to talk to both of us."

"Just think, the two of you could be real sisters some day." Crackers hoots at the thought.

Crackers heads for the boys and leaves me near the fence at the spot where Beverly and I hang out. Maxine's footsteps tromp toward me. Even without realizing, I had her footsteps memorized. They are heavy, like Bigfoot's would be. Boom. Boom. Boom.

"Sorry about your eyes," she says.

She sounds a little sarcastic, but then I remember she always sounds mean, like I'm a worrier, she's a meanie. "Thanks, Maxine."

"Want to go on a swing? I'll push you."

I remember the experiment the Dream Girls did about treating each other the same, regardless of our skin color, or how we feel down deep about them. I don't like Maxine, but I am the person who started the whole "equality" hullaballoo at Crary, and I told Beverly I've forgiven her, so I better give her a real chance. I pose my cane in front of me, like Miss Tyler taught me, but Maxine offers me her arm.

"I saw Beverly and Crackers help you. Tell me how, and I

can guide you to the swings."

"If I hold your arm above your elbow, and you warn me if I need to step up or down or if there's ice, or something, we should be fine."

She leads me over to the swings, and kids say "hi" to us as we walk. The air is cold on my cheeks and my knees, but being outside feels good, even the breeze isn't too bitter.

Maxine places my glove on the swing's chain, and I find my way to the seat and brush the snow off the wooden slat before I sat down.

"Ready?" she shouts from behind me.

"Go slow at first, okay?"

She pushes me slow and easy. The wind whips through my hair, and my stomach does a little twirl with the first uptick of the swing. I picture puffy clouds on blue skies, the kind I love to paint with watercolors—the kind of art that makes you think heaven is in the skies, and God smiles down on you, spreading sunshine on your path.

Back and forth I go, sailing in the sky, letting my imagination take me up, up, and away.

"Hattie! There you are!" Beverly calls.

"I'm swinging!"

Maxine gives me a huge shove then, hard as she can, and I slide right off the swing, flying like a rocket without fuel, and land, plop, in the snow and mud. My knees are covered in muck, but I stand and brush myself off, fighting off the tears stinging the backs of my eyes. I hate Maxine. Even though it's a sin.

"Hattie! Are you all right?"

Beverly's firm grip on my hand holds me steady. "I don't think Maxine knows her own strength."

"That's one possibility."

There was a show on TV one time about a sixth sense. Like you have five senses—touch, taste, sound, sight, smell, but the sixth one is about trusting your gut. Like you have intuition, you can predict something will happen just by feeling it inside, not by some scientific or logical proof. Not knowing based on facts, but on having a premonition. Not necessarily about ghosts or witches or supernatural things like when we play with the Ouija board, but simpler.

I have a strong gut feeling right now. Maxine was up to no good. As usual.

"Let's get outta here. Where's my cane?"

"Hold onto my arm. Your cane's by the leg of the swing set."

We retrieve my cane, and Beverly leads me over to the fence, by our private spot where no one bothers us.

The note! How could I have forgotten?

"I have a note for you. It's from Matt."

"Really?" Her voice tinkles like a bell.

I hand her the note, waiting as patiently as I can, tapping my foot against the snowpack. I can't stand the suspense. "Is there something you want to tell me?"

"Maybe," she says.

I wait, holding my breath. "I want to play the game we used to play."

"Which one?"

"The one where we tell one good thing and one bad thing that happened to us today, but only after you read the note."

Beverly's voice smiles. "Matt and I are going steady."

Acting mad or shocked about Beverly and Matt doesn't make sense, but I can't wrap my brain around them being a couple either. All I can think is "ick." So, I do what comes naturally—go along with her. I'd want her to do the same if I were in her shoes. "When did this happen?"

"Just now. That's my good thing. My bad thing is that I didn't get to you before Maxine pushed you on the swing. I'm really sorry, Hattie."

"That's all right. You know Maxine. She has evil in her blood. She can't help herself. My good thing is you taught me that I could still write, even if I can't see. My mom has a typewriter at home. If she helps me memorize the keyboard, I can type all kinds of stories."

"You can still be an author!"

"I can." Just thinking about writing makes the world all right.

Mrs. Simmons' whistle sounds and Beverly and I make our way to the line.

"Hattie," Mrs. Simmons calls. "Will you lead the class today?"

I'm nervous to lead the class, my first attempt with a cane, but in spite of the swing incident, I'm more confident than ever, so I say, "Sure."

I tap my cane left to right, stepping with the opposite foot, just as Miss Tyler taught me. As we make our way down the hall, Miss Tyler's voice rings out. "Hattie, just who I was coming to see."

She chats with Mrs. Simmons for a second and then I go with her to her little musty office while the rest of the students head back to class. "See you later, Hattie," Beverly says.

"Are you going to tell Crackers the good thing?" I call out to her.

"At lunch," Beverly says. "When the Dream Girls are together."

I smile to myself. I have the best friends in the entire world.

CHAPTER FOURTEEN

MY FIRST BRAILLE CLASS IS ONE OF THE BEST CLASSES I've ever had. I'm stumped when Miss Tyler shows me her typewriter, until I learn it's not a typical typewriter at all, but a Brailler, or a Braille typewriter. When she sets it on the desk in front of me, it clunks, heavy as a box of rocks. "What color is it?"

"Gray, with black keys."

Having an idea of the color helps me make a picture in my head. I put my hands out to examine the contraption. The edges are all rounded. I guess because blind people have a knack for banging into things and they are trying keep the sharp angles to a minimum.

"A Brailler has nine keys, one for each dot of the six in the Braille cell, a space bar, a page advance and a line advance."

I count the keys, only finding eight, but then I think to reach up a little higher and find the ninth. Thoroughness is essential when exploring new things. I also find a couple of knobs.

Miss Tyler hands me a sheet of paper, far thicker than loose-leaf paper. "Braille paper has to be thick so that the indentations made from the keys make raised dots, but don't punch holes through the paper and still maintain their shape."

I guide the paper into the machine, just experimenting, and Miss Tyler watches. I got it. First time. I sit up ramrod tall, like a secretary in front of a typewriter and place my fingers on the six Braille keys.

I learn the alphabet next. One dot for "A" on the left side, closest to the space key. Pressing hard is crucial. If I don't press with enough force, the letter won't show, and no one will be able to read what I'm writing.

"B" is two dots. Key one and two. I'm learning the alphabet fast.

I practiced typing the letters of the alphabet over and over again. Every now and then Miss Tyler reminds me, "Press harder."

"Let's practice reading the letters," she says a good five minutes later.

"How can I read them if I can't see?"

Miss Tyler shows me how to find the top of the page with my fingers, then how to hold a line so I won't lose my place. "Just read the letters, one at a time. Don't worry about the words yet."

"B," I pause and think about the next set of dots. "I. Is it an 'I?' How do I know the difference between an 'A' and an 'I?'"

"Great question! Trust your fingers. You'll learn soon enough."

"What I'm most worried about is being able to read Braille. What if my fingers aren't sensitive enough? What if they don't work?"

"Interestingly enough, I've never had a student whose fingers didn't work. You don't need all your fingers and you'll find over time which fingers are the most adept at reading. Your fingers themselves will tell you."

"Talking fingers." That's funny. "I can't wait to learn everything I can. My friends and I are going to share messages in Braille. Like a secret code." I pause from reading and scratch my head. "I guess we won't have a secret code since I've told you about our plan."

"You're secret is safe with me, Hattie."

"Even after my sight comes back, we can use the code!"

"Even then…" Miss Tyler's voice trails off. "Read to me. We've gone off track."

"I tend to be distractible, even when my eyes work."

I go on reading the letters aloud, spelling out words for Miss Tyler, simple boring baby words like "dog" and "cookie" but I decide Miss Tyler wants me to learn the easy words first.

"You're doing a great job mastering the alphabet. Soon I'll teach you contractions."

"You mean like 'can't' and 'won't'?"

"Braille contractions are a bit different. They're combinations of dots. When they stand alone they represent whole words, rather than individual letters."

"Shorthand?"

"Exactly."

Miss Tyler likes me. I can tell from the tone of her voice.

"Can you give me an example?"

"Of course. There are contractions for words we use often, like the words 'a', 'but', 'every'…"

"I bet there's a contraction for 'the' and 'of', too."

"You'd be correct."

The bell rings, announcing lunch, and Miss Tyler jumps

up from her chair. "Oh my. That was quick. Let's wait for your classmates to come downstairs and then we can retrieve your lunch. It's in your locker, right?"

"We can go now. I have to learn how to go down the hall when other students are there, because life is crowded. I can't hide or only travel places when the world is empty. The world is never empty."

"You're going to be fine, young lady. Just fine."

I don't want Miss Tyler to know how anxious I am to reach the cafeteria and my friends. While I was busy learning Braille my mind didn't wander too much, but since the bell rang, I only think about Beverly revealing her secret to Crackers and me. Going steady with my measly little brother.

Big dust. Big. Big. Dust.

Beverly and Crackers waited for me to start eating. When I make my way to our table, which isn't easy with all the kids milling around, I let out a huge sigh of relief.

I unwrap my sandwich and take a sniff. Liverwurst and mustard.

Beverly interrupts my upturned nose. "Give me your milk money, Dream Girls. I'll get the milk."

I hand over a nickel from my pocket. "Thanks," I say, then call out after her, "Make sure mine's chocolate."

Crackers, in true form, says, "I think we should test you. You sniff everything and tell us what you smell. You can be our official sniff tester."

"Maybe not. Besides, when Beverly comes back from buying our milk, she has big news."

"You mean about the note? You talked to her?"

"Shhh, I didn't tell her I showed you. I don't want her to think I'm nosy."

Crackers slaps me on the back, startling me.

"Hey, I can't see your hand getting ready to swat me. Take it easy, will you?"

I rub my cheek where I bit the inside of my mouth.

"Oops. Sorry, Hattie, blind as a Battie."

Sometimes Crackers is funny. Sometimes she's not.

"Here's your milk," Beverly says. "I put a straw in the carton for you." She puts the carton in my hand and I set it on the table to my right, so I can find it easily.

Beverly scrunches her bony body in next to me and pulls her lunch from her bag. "Darn! Bologna again."

"I have liverwurst. Want to trade?"

"Blech," Crackers says. "That's like eating meat with grit. Or Spam, with globby fat."

"A steady diet of cold hot dogs makes much more sense." I stretch my fingers out in front of me and search her napkin. Sure enough, a plain hot dog with a bite missing, sits in front of her.

Beverly clears her throat.

"Sorry," I say. "Give us the dirt."

"Dirt? Poor choice of words, Hattie," Crackers says.

"We're never going to hear what's up if you keep interrupting."

"I'm not interrupting, you are!"

"Ladies," Beverly says, "do you want to hear my news or not?"

We close our traps and Beverly leans in next to my ear. Crackers bends forward, her breath warm on my face.

"Matt and I are going steady!"

I see Crackers' face scrunch up, even though my eyes don't work. "Details," she says. "Details."

"When we were spending the night at Hattie's and you two went upstairs, Matt came to the basement and played a game of table hockey with me. I kept turning the sticks the wrong way so he came over to help me. When he put his hand on top of mine…"

"Oh, boy!" Crackers snorts. "She's got it bad."

"You didn't kiss him, did you?" I think about kissing a boy someday, but I'm not ready yet. Or am I?

"Not yet," Beverly says, "but if we are going steady, it's just a matter of time." Her voice goes all soft and breathy, like she's a character on General Hospital.

I thought I could keep my opinion to myself, but before I know it, words come sailing out of my mouth. "Personally, I can't imagine what you see in Matt. First of all, he's way younger than you. Second, he's my brother. Third…" I run out of arguments after number two.

"Third," Crackers says, "he's white. Can you imagine the stir you two will cause if anyone finds out? Scandalous, Beverly. You're disgraceful. And everyone thinks you're a sweet genius. Oh, girl, you are trouble!"

I imagine Beverly's big brown eyes. "Crackers," I say. "Tell me. What does Beverly's face look like?"

"She's batting those long, curly eyelashes over her baby browns, and smirking, like she's about to do something ever so naughty."

"I know that look. Beverly, you devil, you."

"How the heck are you two ever going to get together when Matt goes to Catholic school?" Crackers asks.

"I'm hoping Hattie invites me over."

"Great. Now you're using me to get to my brother. I feel so slighted. So…used."

We start giggling. Just like old times. Back when I could see.

The realization hits me out of the blue. Like being struck by a lightning bolt, the flash stabs me and zips through my veins, heating up my blood so I end up feeling like it's evaporated, or been drained right out of me.

Dr. Baker told me before I left the hospital, "You have an advantage, Hattie. Many people are born blind, but you've been able to see for ten years, so those pictures will stay in your mind. You'll remember faces and images of things some folks never have the privilege or opportunity to see."

I should be grateful, but sometimes I miss my eyes.

I remember all the expressions about eyes. *Eyes are the windows to the soul. Beauty is in the eye of the beholder. The apple of my eye.*

I love eyes. Whenever I think about Mom, Dad, Grandma, my brothers, or my friends, the first thing I picture is their eyes. I love how eyes tell you so much about a person. The day Beverly read the horrid note Mrs. Simmons had written, making fun of Beverly's hair and skin color, I first noticed the pain in her eyes. All the life had drained out of them. All the sparkle. Sure, her skin going ashy was another clue, but I knew how sad she was from her eyes. And she wouldn't talk. I worry if something horrible happens to her again, I won't know.

Crackers' face tells me exactly how she's feeling even when she thinks she's wearing a mask and being the class clown. All silly and ridiculous. Sometimes she acts the craziest when she's the saddest. But now I won't be able to tell, because the pain lives way in the back of her eyes. That's where I could spot it.

Mom would probably say I'm having a pity party right now, and she'd probably be right, but hey, I think I'm entitled.

"Hattie." Beverly's voice disrupts my thoughts.

"Hmm?"

"What's wrong?"

"Why do you ask?"

"Your eyes went all blank. Like you might start to cry."

"Nothing's wrong. I was thinking is all."

"Thinking," Crackers says. "Good one, Hattie."

CHAPTER FIFTEEN

CRACKERS WALKS ME HOME IN A BLISTERY WIND. I CAN'T seem to use my cane right, I'm all out of sync with the stepping and the tapping, so I just grip her arm. Plus, the sidewalk is icy, and I'm nervous about falling.

"I'm not joking," Crackers says. "You can't tell your Mom. If she finds out about Matt and Beverly, she'll have a canary. She finally warmed up to the idea of you having a black friend, but once she knows Matt and Beverly are an item, she'll never let Beverly back in your house."

"You're being silly."

"Think, Hattie. Do you know any blacks and whites who are married to each other?"

"No, but I bet there are some couples who are. Isn't Tina Turner married to a white man?"

"Pshaw. Ike Turner is as black as licorice."

"There's some famous singer who's married to a member of another race. Do you know who? I can't think."

"You mean Sammy Davis, Jr. He's married to a model. The blonde."

"Right, that's who I mean. Did you know interracial marriages are illegal in a lot of states?"

"Hattie, are you going to be a politician when you grow up? I thought you were going to be a writer, but you could be the first woman president. The first blind woman president."

"I'm going to be an author, not just a writer, but a bonafide author, which only happens once you've published a book. But when I was talking to my grandma about Martin Luther King, Jr. and his Freedom March, I told her about my dad saying the janitor and the choral teacher at his school were dating. She said blacks and whites can marry each other in some states and not others. How can this be a law? How can who you love be anyone's business but yours?"

"Your grandma is cool."

"She's super cool."

"You should tell her about Beverly and Matt. She'll know what to do."

I trip on a raised edge of the sidewalk, slide on the ice and pull Crackers down on top of me. She starts laughing, of course. "Good job changing the subject, Hattie." Her voice comes from over my head. "Here, let me help you stand up."

Trying to stand up is like having roller skates on for the first time. I keep slipping and sliding all over the place, my legs splaying in opposite directions. My hands slither across the snow and ice and I can't find anything to grip onto so I can get my legs under me. My knee begins to throb where I went down, and my side aches.

"Grab my hand."

"I can't see, you idiot. I have no idea where your hand is."

"Let's not get testy," Crackers says.

Anger bites at the back of my throat. "You think this is easy, being blind? Fine. Let's trade. You be the one in the dark for a change. See how you like it."

Crackers grips me under my arm and her foot stops in front of mine. "I can lever you up if you'll cooperate. Stop being so darned stubborn and stand up."

I do as she tells me, the weight of the day more than I can stand.

She wraps me in a giant hug and holds me. "I'm sorry, Hattie. If I could, I would have made it to you before those kids knocked you off your bike. I should have been there. I should have protected you."

Now we are hugging. "No. My blindness is not your fault. Sure, I wish this hadn't happened to me. I'm having a bad day is all."

"You've been really brave today. I don't know if I could be as brave as you."

"You are way tougher than me."

"Am not," Crackers says as we inch down the street.

"Are." I squeeze her hand. "Beverly might be the bravest of us. She puts up with tons of teasing about being black, forgives the haters, wants to marry a white man, and she's way smarter than the two of us put together."

"Can you imagine how cute their kids would be?" Crackers asks.

"Ick. Thinking about that is gross. Totally nauseating."

"Matt has all those freckles and red hair. Beverly has those huge eyes and she's so dainty and pretty. I hope they have a girl. She'll come out milk chocolate, with Matt's freckles and Beverly's thick hair."

"Her hair makes me so jealous. I wish my hair was like hers."

"I want to get one of those hair straighteners like we saw when we went to her house."

"You like to play with contraptions, but you'd probably burn off your hair with a hot comb. Those aren't made for white folks like us."

"White folks," Crackers says. "You're funny, Hattie."

"One thing good about being blind?"

"What would that be, Sugar Pea?"

"I can't tell what color people are. If there's one way to eliminate racism, this is it."

"Very logical solution, Hattie. Make everyone blind."

"Give me a little credit. It would work."

"Even though you can't see, you still worry about racism?"

"Just because my eyes went wonky doesn't mean I'm not the same person. I can't wait to learn Braille, so I can read again, and Beverly showed me how I could still write, so I can write stories even before I learn Braille. Once I learn how to write Braille, I'll learn how to read, too, then I'll type all my stories so I can read things over. I'm hoping to write to Martin Luther King, Jr. again and tell him what happened to me. I don't want his pity, but I want him to know I'll continue to fight for equal rights, no matter what people do to me. He's willing to go to jail, or be killed for what he believes in. I am too."

"Hattie!" Crackers says.

"What?"

We giggle as we step up the slippery driveway to my back door. My hand glides over the knob but the door sticks as I swing it open and bashes me right between the eyes.

Mom screams from the other side of the door. "Hattie,

watch what you're doing!"

I must have sliced the bridge of my nose pretty good, or my forehead, because I taste blood on my lips.

Crackers whispers, "You scare me sometimes."

I'm not sure if she's talking to my mom or me. But in my mind, Mom is the scary one right now.

"You need stitches," Mom blurts out.

"Good thing it's so cold out, Mrs. Percha. I think Hattie's head is frozen. She should be crying, but she isn't."

Mom must be giving Crackers a look, because the back hall goes totally silent. She's probably screwing up her face in a "don't challenge me, young lady" way, her eyes beady with anger and frustration.

"Hold this on her head," she orders.

Crackers whirls me around and tells me to sit down on the back step, then whispers. "Here's a washcloth. Put pressure on your cut. We won't tell her about your knee."

"Where am I bleeding?"

Crackers pulls off my gloves and tells where me to find the wound. I discover a slice in my forehead. With my fingers, I feel the sticky blood, and the deep cut.

The half bath is right off the back hall, and Crackers goes inside and turns on the water. When she comes out, she says, "I'll wash off your knee. The blood dried pretty fast, maybe it's frozen on there."

We both giggle softly, but as I warm up, I start to ache and my head begins throbbing.

"Mom," I call. "Just put a butterfly bandage on my head. I don't need stitches."

"But you'll have a scar," she says.

"Will I?" I ask Crackers.

"Battle scars are cool," she says.

The last thing I want is stitches, but scarring my face when I already have a major problem with my eyes doesn't seem like a good thing either. The way I'm going, I might wind up looking like Frankenstein's monster, with stitch marks all over my body.

"Your mom cracks me up," Crackers says.

"How?"

"She told you to watch where you're going. How can you do that when you can't see?"

"I need a fairy godmother."

"What? Are you feeling okay? Did you knock yourself silly?"

"I feel awful, but if I had a fairy godmother, maybe she could make me see again. A miracle would be good right now."

CHAPTER SIXTEEN

MOM DOESN'T TAKE MUCH CONVINCING. SHE PLACES an adhesive butterfly bandage on my forehead, hands me an ice pack and runs off to change Larry's stinky diaper. Matt strolls into the kitchen two minutes later searching out a snack.

"Hey, Crackers," he says. "How's it going?"

"Cool. How 'bout you?"

"I'm cool."

These two take my mind off the pounding in my head. Matt must be one of those kids who was born ahead of his time. When I listen to him, he sounds like a teenager, the way he has the world by the tail. Then again, Grandma sometimes says I'm an old soul. Maybe it runs in the family.

"Hattie," he says, all nonchalant like. "Got anything for me?"

"Oh, yeah. In my school bag. In the back hall."

His footsteps fly out of the room and Crackers opens and

closes cupboards. "Where does your mom keep the cookies?"

"There might be some Oreos in the cupboard next to the stove."

"We need a snack. Sugar helps when you have an injury."

If I didn't have Crackers in my life, I'd be wailing right now. "Hey, we should have read the note Beverly wrote Matt."

"Hattie, Hattie, Hattie. Knocking your head changed you. You've said more crazy stuff in the last five minutes than you have in your entire life."

She sets the Oreo pack in front of me, as well as a glass of milk. "If you're a dunker, hold your glass and then dip your head so you don't drip all over the place."

"I know how to eat. Mostly, anyway." Lucky for me, I'm not a dunker, and I know how to check how full my glass is with my finger, so at least I won't have an accident in the next five minutes. "Why do you think I'm crazy?"

"You would never read someone's private notes before, and now, twice in one day, you want to spy on people."

"I wonder if they kissed and Beverly didn't want to tell us. They could have made a secret pact."

"I know he's your brother, but Matt's cute."

"But he's younger than her."

"But he's tall," Crackers says, "so he seems older. And he acts older than his age, too."

"I'm worried about that."

"You're worried about what?" Mom strolls into the kitchen, toting Larry on her hip.

My heart about stops in my chest. I have to pay better attention. If Mom gets word of Matt and Beverly, she'll have a conniption for sure. "Nothing. We're just talking."

She plops Larry in my lap and says, "Keep an eye on your

brother, will you?"

"Matt," she says next. "What are you doing?"

Crackers and I hold our collective breath. Larry squirms in my lap and tangles his sticky fingers in my hair.

"What do you have on your hands, little boy?" I stand, hitching Larry up on my hip, rehearsing the number of steps to the sink in my head.

"I can take him," Crackers says.

"No, I want to do this. I have to be able to do things for myself. And for my brother."

"Stubborn girl," Crackers chortles.

I take small, tentative steps, but I make my way over to the sink and balance Larry on the counter, one hand resting on his knee while I turn on the faucet and wet a washcloth with the other. I wipe his hands. "I don't even want to know what is on your hands."

He leans over and I feel his leg slipping out of my grasp. "Help!"

Crackers catches him at the last minute and lifts Larry into her arms. "You are so cute."

I about hyperventilate. "Thank you," I whisper.

"No problem, Miss Do-It-Yourself."

Matt saunters in. "What's for dinner?"

"Smells like Mom has spaghetti on the stove. Can't you tell?"

"I guess," he says. "I'm going to go upstairs for a few minutes and answer the note."

"Carry on," Crackers says and she must have tossed him an Oreo, because she adds, "Here. Eat this."

Mom steps into the kitchen. "What note?"

"Oh, nothing," Crackers, Matt and I say in unison.

Mom's inhaling sharply now. She knows we're a bunch of fibbers. "I can't wait until you're all in high school. You will be the death of me."

"Can I ask a question, Mrs. Percha?" Crackers turns on her syrupy, sweet voice when she tries to butter up my mom.

"What is it?"

"I noticed you told Hattie to watch where she's going, and to keep an eye on Larry. Do you think you should talk about her eyes like that when she can't see?"

My turn to inhale a sharp breath. My ribs clench as I wait for Mom to answer.

"We see with more than our eyes, Ann. We see with our hands and our ears and our fingers and our hearts. Hattie can still see. Her eyes are only one of the ways she used to see."

"Makes perfect sense. Thanks for explaining."

Crackers reminds me of Eddie Haskell, the character on the TV show, Leave It to Beaver. He's always asking Mrs. Cleaver inappropriate things, or being plain old goofy, but she tolerates him because he's so polite. Charming—in a totally sympathetic way. I wish I could do the same as Crackers, without even thinking, too. I have to go over things in my head a million times, practicing over and over again to make sure I say things the right way because I'm worried about offending someone. Crackers' and Eddie Haskell's approach seems so much simpler. This little voice tells me even if I try my hardest, I'll never be able to pull it off. Not in this lifetime.

I'm grateful to Crackers for asking Mom about referring to my eyes so much when she talks to me. I wondered the same thing, and to be honest, heat brewed in my belly when she told me to watch where I was going. But she's right. I can still see, just not in the way I'm used to. And she's finally stopped stammering when she talks about my eyes. I'll admit it. Her honesty is a relief.

Being blind is going to be different, but not impossible. Not every minute at least.

CHAPTER SEVENTEEN

MATT PUTS ME UP TO ASKING MOM IF I CAN HAVE another sleepover with Beverly and Crackers. He figures since Mom feels sorry for me lately, she'll say yes. I tell him I'd rather have them over to Grandma's house, but he disagrees. He has ulterior motives—he wants to see Beverly, his girlfriend. Ugh.

But he's right. Mom agrees in an instant—times have changed.

Saturday night comes in a flash. We're in the basement with our sleeping bags, snacks, and the portable record player. Beverly has the new Supremes album…and we're singing into saltshakers, our microphones, trying to figure out harmonies.

Matt tromps downstairs, strumming the strings of his guitar to let us know he's here.

"Hey," Beverly says.

She never used to say "hey." She's changed so much the past few days. When I touch her hair, it's smooth against her head, no more pigtails with clips. Her mom irons and curls her hair. I'm sure she looks quite sophisticated with her new style. Crackers even commented about the blush on her cheeks.

"Are you wearing makeup?" I ask.

"Mom let me use a little mascara."

"I bet you're beautiful."

Matt takes a seat in the folding chair and strums along while we sing. Beverly's voice sounds like a heavenly angel. She could be a Supreme herself when she gets older. No wonder Matt's in love with her.

Crackers clutches my arm and yells in my ear over the music, "Let's give these lovebirds a minute."

"The laundry room," I say. "We can hang out there."

She leads me into the laundry room and we pile some towels onto the concrete floor and sit across from each other, Indian style.

"Should we listen? He's going to try to get to first base."

I ignore her. I have other more important questions on my mind. "Have you ever kissed a boy?" I ask.

"No way, Jose! I'm sure I'll meet some dreamy guy some day, but I don't have anyone in mind."

"George Harrison is my crush," I confess before sadness seeps into my pores. "The Dream Girls are changing."

"What do you mean?" Crackers fiddles with clothespins she's found on the line, snapping them opened and closed.

"I always wanted to change the world with our club, and I guess we sort of did when we did the brown hair/blond hair exercise in our class. But now Beverly dreams about boys. She won't care about changing the world anymore."

"Is your beloved Martin Luther King, Jr. married?"

"Yes," I say.

"Well then, Beverly can have a boyfriend. She won't stop doing things because she's in love." She draws out the words "in love," as she says them. "You have to treat everyone equally, Hattie. Practice what you preach."

"You're right. I guess I don't want to lose her to Matt."

"You won't. She might be all googly-eyed for a while, but she'll come down to earth eventually."

The light snaps on. "Are we sitting in the dark?" I ask.

"Yes," Mom says. "What's going on here?"

"Nothing at all, Mrs. Percha." Crackers uses her syrupy sweetness on Mom. "Hattie and I came in her to find some clothespins. Matt wants to accompany our singing on the guitar, and we are going to clip his music to the stand so he doesn't lose his place."

Crackers' line works. She clicks the clothespins together, proof of what we were doing in the laundry room.

My heart hammers in my chest. I have to pay better attention. Why didn't I hear Mom on the stairs? Thank goodness the laundry room is right off the steps before the rec room. If mom saw Beverly and Matt alone, all "H," "E," double hockey sticks would have broken out. I make a mental note to tell Crackers we have to be more alert. Even when I could see, I paid attention to things like this. What's wrong with me?

Mom gathers a load of wash from off the floor, tosses the dirty clothes into the washer, and starts the machine.

"That was a close one," I whisper to Crackers as we troop back to the rec room. "We have to listen for my parents. They could be anywhere at any time."

Crackers grips my elbow as we turn the corner into the rec room. "They're kissing!" she hisses.

I miss my eyes more than ever. I want to see this!

"Are they all mushy?"

"Oh yeah," she says under her breath.

They must not be able to hear us over the music. I clear my throat, and call out, "We found the clothespins."

Wha…?" Matt says.

"Mom's down here doing laundry. You might want to get back to playing guitar, unless you're up for a heap of trouble," Crackers warns.

"You guys won't be the first mixed couple in the world, but you're headed for disaster if Mom finds out. She'll have a cow. Right here. Right now."

"She won't find out. Not unless you blab."

Beverly stays quiet for a long minute. "Don't worry, Hattie. Everything will be okay."

An idea sparks. I can change the world by helping Beverly and Matt fight prejudice about their relationship. This is the best idea I've had in a long time. Something to fight for. A way to make the world a better place.

"Uh-oh," Crackers says. "Look at Hattie. Her brain is on fire again. Watch out world!"

"What?" I ask, trying to feign innocence.

Mom's slippers shuffle into the room. "Matt," she says. "Upstairs. Now."

"Be there in a minute," he says, casually ignoring her.

"Now!" she shouts.

My hand goes over my mouth and I hear Crackers, "tsk, tsk, tsk."

"Do what your mom asks, Matt," Beverly says.

Beverly's right. This is the exact wrong time to challenge Mom. If she saw or heard something, she's going to get angrier if he disobeys.

We gather in a circle on my sleeping bag and grip hands. "What will she say? What will she do if she saw us kissing? Will she make me go home? Will she call my mom?"

Talk about having a canary. Beverly acts like a criminal caught with her hand in the till.

"Mom will definitely not be in favor of kissing. She thinks girls who kiss when they are young will become tramps. It's not her fault, it's how she was raised."

"You are far too understanding, Hattie."

"I don't agree with her, I'm just telling you how my mom is. Remember how she didn't want me to be friends with you because you're black? She came around once she had a chance to get used to the idea. She'll be as concerned about the kissing as she will about the fact that you are black and Matt is white."

"I understand. I'm sure my mom wouldn't approve of me kissing a boy. And I'm positive my dad would arrest me and throw me in jail."

"My dad would have a heart attack," Crackers says. "But that's because he expects me to tackle boys, not kiss them."

"Tackling boys can be taken a number of different ways," I tease.

Crackers punches me in the arm.

"Yeah," Beverly says. "Maybe that's why you like sports so much. Close, personal contact."

"Hardly. Boys are gross."

The smell of popcorn wafts down the stairs. "I'll go up for the snacks," I say. "Then I can spy—see how Matt's doing."

I grip the handrail and climb the steps, halting in the back hall when I hear Mom's voice. "Do you have any idea what you're doing? You're far too young to be kissing a girl. And a black girl? What could you be thinking? This kind of behavior is completely unacceptable."

The door is open, so I walk into the kitchen, acting like I haven't heard a word.

"Do I smell popcorn?"

"Not now," Mom says, the edge in her voice slicing like a cleaver. "Come to think of it, join us for a minute."

I make my way toward them, pull the seat away from the table and slink into a chair. Reaching out for Matt's hand under the table, I give him a squeeze, pretending I haven't overheard the conversation. "What's up?"

"Matt and Beverly were kissing. You know how I feel about kissing at such a young age, and then there is the whole race issue to consider."

"What race issue?" I play dumb.

"Mixed couples don't do well."

"Do you know any?" I'm acting like a devil's advocate right now, stirring up trouble. I know she doesn't know any mixed couples. Dad does, the janitor and choral teacher at his school, but Mom? No way.

"Hattie, please don't interrupt."

I zip my mouth shut and wait. Mom ignores my question. "Life is hard enough without falling in love with a member of another race. And children, should they come along, will be the subject of endless rebuke."

"Rebuke?"

"Teasing, bullying, taunting. Like you and your friends went through, Hattie. Your confrontation with those hateful kids cost you your vision. Would you want something similar to happen with Beverly or Matt?"

"They aren't getting married. They just kissed."

"I need to talk to your dad about this."

"Okay. Can I get some popcorn?"

Mom doesn't answer me.

"She can't see you nodding, Mom," Matt says.

"Yes," Mom says. I think she's still breathing, but I'm not sure.

Matt pours and salts some popcorn and hands a bowl to me. "I'll bring down some Coke."

"You'd better not."

"I thought you were all about changing the world, Sis. You can't say one thing, then back away from what you believe because you're scared about how someone might react."

"Guess I'm not the only rabble-rouser around this place."

"Definitely not."

CHAPTER EIGHTEEN

D AD CALLS MATT AND ME DOWN ON SUNDAY MORNING after church. We gather around the coffee table in the den, a tiny room with a love seat, which barely fits between the door and the wall, and butts up against a worn upholstered chair. The chair hits against the TV stand. If the room didn't have two windows, we'd call it a closet.

I finger the braided rug while I sprawl on the floor and wait for Dad to start the conversation.

"Mom told me about the kissing last night. I've already spoken to Matt privately, but I wanted to talk to the two of you as well. Mom is quite concerned, not only about Matt and Beverly's ages, but also about the complications that accompany an interracial relationship."

I love how Dad talks to us like we're adults.

Matt goes first. "I don't believe people should consider skin color when choosing a mate. I'm not saying that I'm ready to get married. I've barely started dating."

This is a total crack up. Matt's nine years old. What's he going to be like when he's eleven? Does he think he'll have a driver's license by then? A job? His own apartment? I can't help giggling.

I wish I could see Dad's face. I'm sure he's trying as hard as he can not to smile, or laugh, or raise his brows. But he also knows and understands us. There are times when he raises just one eyebrow at Matt, like he admires how spunky Matt is. But in a situation like this, he'll take what he knows and use his knowledge to guide and help us. He can't help it. He's a teacher.

"But if I happen to fall in love with a black girl, I'll marry her, no question about it."

"Admirable stance, son, and I applaud your courage and conviction. There are further considerations though. As a musician, I have some experience with interracial marriages. A few of my band mates are married to members of a different race. They've learned to develop thicker skins—folks turn their noses up when they see them. Avoid them. Glare at them as if they have leprosy. Tolerating an overwhelming lack of respect can take a toll after a while. We all want to be accepted. Those of my friends who have kids are quick to admit how much harder life is for their children. They are called vicious names, snubbed, and mistreated in every way imaginable. I'm talking about horrible cruelty."

I think about Beverly and her family. They deal with bigotry every day. It must be awful to be treated like garbage because your skin is dark. I have problems, but I'm still white, so people don't treat me poorly. It's just not fair what blacks have to put up with. "The world needs to change. People with courage, like your friends, will make the world better," I say. "Since I'll be going to sixth grade next year, and then junior high, I should start thinking of ways to change people's minds now, before I go to high school and my generation starts dating."

"I agree, Hattie. The world needs to change. But changing your classmates' minds at school about being friends with members of the opposite race took a horrific incident and your intervention. People rarely question what they were raised to believe. This is no easy task."

"Dad," Matt says, "I want to go to Crary. St. Mary's doesn't have enough diversity."

Matt's trademark is his perfect posture, his soldier straight shoulders and solid stance. I picture him sitting upright, locking Dad's brown eyes with his hazel ones, stubborn as a sticky zipper.

"Crary isn't an option for you right now. You'll be an SMR student until the end of this school year. I'm not negotiating. Next year, we might be willing to consider a change."

"If I attend public school, you'll save my tuition. Hattie's proven she can learn as much, if not more, in a public school. Plus, if I went to Crary, I could help Hattie out."

"I don't need help. My vision will be back by next year."

All the oxygen leaves the room.

"You may think I'm being a dreamer, but my eyes could heal. And even if they don't, I'll make the best of things. You've always said I shouldn't let hardships stand in my way. And I don't need Matt's help."

"You let Crackers and Beverly help you." Matt's voice fills with accusation.

"That's different."

"I don't see how."

I don't have a decent explanation to offer, but I know one thing. I want to be like everyone else. No matter what happens with my eyes.

Dad interrupts us. "You're handling things very well, Hattie, and I respect your independence and courage. But we're getting off topic. Here's the bottom line. I don't want you kissing girls, Matt. You're far too young. Dating at your age…"

I think Dad is about to say "silly," but he stops himself.

"…it's unnecessary. There will be plenty of time for girls when you're a teenager."

"Is Mom still mad about Percha's Dating Service?" Matt asks.

"Not really. But we do want you to pursue interests more appropriate to your age. You're an excellent athlete and a fine student. Take some time to learn about life before you have a girlfriend."

"How old were you when you had your first girlfriend?" Matt asks.

My ears perk up. This should be good.

"I was eleven."

"So you weren't in your teens?" Matt wants his way. He'll try anything to make his point.

"Two years away from you, son, if you decide you really need and want a girlfriend. And quite honestly, if I was Beverly's parent, I wouldn't want my ten-year-old daughter going steady."

"You don't approve of her choices?" Matt won't give up. Ever.

Dad chuckles. "She has excellent taste, and I see, between her love of music and yours why you're drawn to each other. Just slow down. There's no rush. Just be friends."

"I had no idea Beverly was so fast." The words slip out of my mouth before I realize.

"Fast?"

We all know what "fast" means, but I change the subject. "We had to run the mile for school. She beat everyone in our class!"

"Even Crackers?" Dad asks.

"No, everyone but Crackers."

CHAPTER NINETEEN

TWO WEEKS LATER, GRANDMA AND I HEAD TO DR. Baker's office for my follow-up visit. Mom wanted to take me, but Larry has been barfing since midnight, and Mom decided she couldn't leave him with Grandma. I'm sure Grandma's been barfed on before, but Mom believes she should clean up her own kid's vomit, so I'm sitting in the front seat of Grandma's bright red Mustang, listening to the Beatles on the radio.

Grandma turns down the volume. "How are you, Hattie?"

"I'm doing great. Braille's the coolest language, and Miss Tyler ordered all my textbooks for me, so I can read and follow along. She says I'm a fast learner. I even wrote a story the other night. Mom let me bring her typewriter to my room so I could type, but I can't read back to myself. When I'm older, I'm going to develop a machine that can read back what I've written.

"What do you think, Grandma?"

"About?"

"What if I'm always blind?"

"What if you are? You're no different than you ever have been. Here's the thing, Hattie, we all have something holding us back. Your blindness is on the outside, but even people with healthy eyes have some kind of roadblock they're dealing with."

"You mean like Mom doesn't change her mind easily because she's scared of new things?"

"Why yes, that's a perfect example." Grandma pats my knee, pride evident in her touch.

"And Crackers became a class clown because laughing is better than crying about missing her mom."

"Laughter is a way of escaping pain. While Crackers' heartache doesn't show on the outside, she carries the loss of her mom with her, wherever she goes. She'll always miss her mom and the memories they would have made together."

"Mom drives me crazy sometimes, but I can't imagine my life without her. She's always there for me when I'm sick, she loves me even when she's mad at me, and just knowing I have her makes me feel safe."

"Crackers and her dad are close, but there's no substitute for a mom."

"Who will teach her girl stuff like makeup and boyfriends?"

"You and Beverly."

"You're right. Like Crackers lost her mom and I lost my vision, but we can help each other deal with what we lack by filling in the gaps."

"You're a very insightful young lady, honey. There's more too. Remember when Crackers told you about her mom dying when she was so young? Your heart went out to her. You were sorry for her, and sad. But she never wanted your sympathy, did she?"

"No, she blew me off. Like losing her mom happened a long time ago and she was over her death, but you can't ever get over something so important."

"Her life changed the day she lost her mom. She feels the loss, sometimes her heart breaks all over again, but she has to make her way through the days, so she's appointed herself the class clown—her role is to cheer everyone up, to make them happy in spite of the fact that her own heart has been permanently scarred. That's how she copes."

"I wonder if she was funny before her mom died."

"I don't know, but she's found a way to negotiate and manage her life in a positive way. Some folks see themselves as victims when they suffer a tragedy. Some folks are survivors. Crackers decided to be a survivor."

"You are too, aren't you, Grandma? I heard Mom and Dad talk about how you had cancer when Mom was small."

"I'm proud to call myself a survivor."

"Do you mind telling me about being sick? Were you scared you would die?"

"Frightened beyond words. Your mother was only five years old. Grandpa had his job, so your mom had to stay with her grandma, Grandma Hattie, who you were named for, while I went through rounds of radiation. Your mom was so sad—she didn't want me to leave her. I struggled to explain my illness. I knew she would worry whether or not I would come back to her if I told her too much. Yet, she was also too young to understand, and only knew I was saying goodbye. I didn't do the best job of helping her through a very difficult time."

"But you were sick. How could you?" Poor Grandma, having to leave her precious daughter to go off for treatment, and not even knowing if she'd recover.

"At the time, the outlook was poor. Between us, I'm the lone survivor. The treatment was experimental. All the other women in my group lost the fight...." Her voice trails off, and I imagine her thinking about her friends through the sorrow in her voice as she remembers them. Turns out, Grandma is stronger than I ever knew. No wonder she's so wise.

"I'm sorry, Grandma."

"Cancer taught me countless lessons. I learned to value each and every day. I celebrate the small stuff. Appreciate the little things. Never feel sorry for me, Hattie."

"You're really strong."

"The tough times make you stronger. If life went along like a happy little tune, you'd never have courage to fight, never want for more, never learn how deep you can go. When you think you can't weather one more hardship, you learn that you are far stronger than you ever dreamed. Whether your vision comes back or not, you'll always have your heart and soul."

"Did you ever feel sorry for yourself?"

"Of course. That's just human nature. Making adjustments scares us silly. We can't help but want what we no longer have, but that doesn't mean we can't lead full lives. Nothing will stop us, Hattie. Nothing."

We pull into Dr. Baker's parking lot. Grandma doesn't hit the curb like Mom does, but I can tell she's slowing down, and we're about to receive some news. If I can only be as strong as Grandma.

CHAPTER TWENTY

D R. Baker's nurse takes me back to the ophthalmoscope, the giant machine that sees behind my eyes. I hold out hope for good news—my eyes are healing, my retinas are reattaching—but even as Dr. Baker eases my chin into the felt-lined cup, I know what he will find.

"Hmm," Dr. Baker says.

If my eyes were healing, he would have a lilt to his voice, not a simmering, sorry tone.

I swallow over the stone in my throat, trying to be brave, but I can't hold back, and my eyes start to water. Doc passes me a tissue so I can wipe them. He can't see what's going on if my tears are in the way.

"No progress yet, I'm afraid," he says. "This doesn't mean you won't recover some of your sight, and things look fairly good. Your eyes are healing well. Let's take another look in a month. If you find something changes before then, have your mother call the office and set up an appointment. I'm sorry to make you wait longer, but this is how things go some times."

"Will anyone ever invent an eye transplant?"

"I sure hope so."

"I'd like to be the first patient to receive one."

"I'll be sure to let you know, young lady."

He rests a heavy hand on my shoulder. I decide I can be blind for another month. And since I have no choice, I vow to practice Braille on my stylus so I can read what I write.

Grandma takes me out for a hot fudge sundae at Sanders on our way home. The ice cream is cool on my dusty throat and the scent of chocolate helps me shed the awful antiseptic smell of the doctor's office. I'd like to chat with Grandma about regular things, like Crackers' latest tricks at school, but I can't concentrate. My world seems dark and murky, like a never-ending stormy night.

"You can do this," she says. "Not every day will be easy, but you have so many people who love and support you. Give yourself time to adjust."

"How long will it take before I wrap my head around being blind for the rest of my life?"

"No one can say. It's your decision."

I wish someone would tell me, "By next Tuesday, you'll be ready to tackle the world."

If I had an idea, then I could make plans. But instead I start wondering how I can be a blind author, how much I'll miss playing basketball with Crackers, how I'll feel when Matt can drive a car and I can't.

"You're allowed to be sad, Hattie."

I bite back tears. I'm sick of feeling sorry for myself. "I'm worried mostly. What if I don't remember what you look like?"

"You'll never forget. Your grandpa has been gone for a few

years now, and I can still hear his voice and see the twinkle in his eyes when he smiled."

"I don't want people to feel sorry for me. Will Mom cry when we tell her?"

"Probably. But she'll be crying because she wishes she could be the one who is blind. She'll cry because she never wants you to suffer. She knows you will manage because you're of strong stock, but she still wants to protect you. All parents feel that way. Dad will be sad, too. And your brothers and friends. I know you don't want their sympathy, just like Crackers didn't want yours when she told you about her mom.

"What you want is people's understanding and compassion. And you want their help from time to time. You're an independent girl, Hattie, so you'll have to learn to ask for help. Some people see needing a hand as weakness, but you'll learn there is courage in knowing when to ask for help, and solace in having friends who offer you a hand seamlessly, without you even having to tell them."

Every time Grandma shares her nuggets of wisdom, my heart swells with hope, like I can do this. I mean, she had cancer and survived. Crackers lost her mom and she's still laughing. Beverly is black and treated poorly because of it, but she never stops living her life and going after what she wants. Mom overcame Grandma having cancer and met Dad and has a family.

I have to remember this. Everyone has something to deal with. Something they are trying to overcome. Whether it's noticeable, like my eyes being messed up, or invisible, like Crackers being motherless, everyone has something.

The more I think about this, the more I think about Martin Luther King, Jr. He knows we are all the same on the inside, no matter what the color of our skin, the size of our family, our challenges that don't show, or he wouldn't be trying to change the world.

The Beatles come on the radio, a song by George Harrison, my secret crush. I wonder if Mom will let me get the new Beatles album.

Mom waits by the side door, rustling her hands on her apron as we walk inside. For once, I'm glad I can't see, because if I saw the worry etched in her eyes, I'd break down.

"Let's go in the kitchen and have a cup of tea," Grandma suggests.

Mom's really smart, so I know she already figured out my news, but she goes along with us anyway and puts the kettle on to boil. The teapot whistles a few minutes later.

"How many spoons of sugar would you like, Hattie?" she asks, a false lilt to her voice.

"Two, please, and some milk." I actually prefer milk and sugar with a spot of tea.

I decide to deliver the news myself, instead of letting Grandma pave the way. "My eyes aren't any better. They might improve in the future, but for the meantime, I can't see."

All the air disappears from the room and a stretched silence replaces the oxygen.

"I'm sort of getting used to being blind," I say. "I hope my eyes heal, but if they don't, I'll be all right."

Mom lays her hand atop mine, and my heart breaks right down the middle. But I refuse to give in to my sadness. It's oozed out enough. Time to put on a brave face and carry on. Life could be so much worse.

CHAPTER TWENTY-ONE

"RISE AND SHINE, HATTIE." MOM'S VOICE BREAKS into my dream. I prop up on my elbow and rub my eyes.

"What? I thought I could sleep in on Saturday."

"I have a nice surprise for you. Mr. McCracken called after you went to bed last night and he's invited you to go sledding at Rouge Park with the girls, then take you all to Howard Johnson afterward for hot chocolate."

"Can I take the Yankee Clipper?" We have a toboggan and a saucer sled and the Yankee Clipper, which is my all-time favorite, because I can make sharp turns while I'm riding.

"I offered Mr. McCracken any of our sleds."

This is the first time Crackers has invited me to do something with her family. I've only met her dad a few times. Once when Grandma and I dropped Crackers off at home after a visit to Beverly's house, and then again at the police station and when he brought Crackers for the overnight, but I don't know him. Jitters fill my belly.

"Hurry up. Get dressed," Mom says. "I've brought up your leggings, so put them on here, then we'll have a quick breakfast so you're ready on time."

I pull on a pair of long johns, a pair of pants, a long-sleeved shirt and a sweater. After I think for a minute, I decide to double up on socks too. I hate cold feet.

"Beverly's coming?"

"You betcha." Mom's cheery this morning.

Two months ago, Mom would never have allowed this, much less been happy to see us out in public together.

Crackers told me her dad works with a lot of black men at Ford, so he probably doesn't even know some people don't like black and white kids hanging out together.

I scarf down my Malt-O-Meal and orange juice, sweat beading on my forehead. Might have been a better idea to put on my leggings right before I headed out the door.

A car beeps in the driveway and five seconds later there's a rap on the door. "Hattie!" Crackers voice hollers. "Time for fun!"

I open the door to her shouting, "Can you dig it? Dad's taking us to the park."

"I can dig it."

Mom gives me a peck on the cheek and shoves me out the door, instructing Matt to load the sleds in Mr. McCracken's trunk.

Crackers grabs my hand and drags me into the back seat. Beverly is already there, and scoots over when I climb in the car. "Hattie, Hattie! This is the best day."

I whisper to Beverly, "Matt says hi." She squeezes my hand.

"Hi, Mr. McCracken," I stop and say.

"Howdy do, Hattie!"

No surprise. He's as funny as Crackers.

The ride to the park passes in a flash. Before long, we are at the top of the hill, a fine snowfall brushing our cheeks as we linger, deciding the best trail to try.

"The one on the right is the iciest. We might want to try that first. We'll fly down!" Crackers says.

"Or," I offer, "we could start easy. Try a snow-covered trail out in the open. The one through the trees is hard sometimes, unless you're good at piloting a sled."

"Huh," Crackers says. "I'm shocked you don't have more faith in me. Here's an idea. We pile on. Hattie, I should go on the bottom, because then I can steer. You next, because you're the heaviest next to me. Beverly, you're on top, because you're the lightest. Weight, that is."

Beverly titters. "Not the lightest. You're hilarious, Crackers."

We pile on while Mr. McCracken sits at a nearby picnic table and lights a cigarette. I can smell the tobacco burning.

I'm holding onto Crackers' shoulders for dear life. Beverly lies on top of me, and we all count. "One, two, three, ready, set…"

Mr. McCracken dashes over and gives the sled a swift push from behind, yelling, "Land Ho!"

Funny, since we're already on land.

The wind hits my face full force and we sail through the snow, speeding down the hill faster than an arrow. "Woo-hoo!" I yell.

"Hold on tight," Crackers shouts, "there's a bump coming."

Beverly screams in my ear. "This is the most fun ever!"

Then we hit the bump. Turns out to be more than a bump

though—more like a cliff. We are soaring through the air. I can't hear the runners shushing over the ice any longer, just the sound of the wind rushing past us. I'm praying for a smooth landing as I picture the three of us, still holding on to each other with all our might, and how we must look.

Crackers begins shrieking. Beverly joins her. I don't know whether to be scared or excited, but I whoop along with them.

A sudden jolt and we're down, heaped on top of each other like ragdolls, laughing and hugging.

"Cool," I say and we tromp back up the hill. "My favorite part of sledding is steering. Can I try this time? You can ride on my back, Beverly or Crackers, and grab the bar if I misunderstand your directions."

"Great idea," Beverly says. "I'll ride on your back and Crackers can go first on the saucer and carve a path for us."

"Yippee, Hattie's back in the driver's seat." Crackers shoots ahead to grab the saucer and plops down in front of us at the top of the hill. "I'm going to curl up on the saucer so I can do some spins, so give me a head start so we don't crash."

Beverly giggles, like we would never crash, but I know better. Our luck, we would run right over Crackers—flatten her like a pancake, or an animal rug.

I lay down on the sled and Beverly positions herself on top of me, placing her hands over mine on the steering bar. "Let me try. Tell me which way to turn."

"Okey dokey," Beverly says. "Mr. McCracken is talking to someone. We're on our own. Push us off."

I dig my feet into the snow and grip the ground with my boots, pushing as hard as I can to give us some speed as we head down the hill.

We're off and the snow flies in my face.

"Turn, Hattie, turn."

"Which way?" I holler back.

"Left."

I cut the bar to the left.

"The other left, Hattie. Your right."

I push the bar up to the other side.

"Hang on!" Beverly shouts in my ear. She shoves my hands off the bar, and rights the sled before we topple to the side and roll down the hill.

"Holy smokes," Crackers yells from below. "You two are dangerous."

I slip and slide as I try to stand, and find a firm hand gripping my arm. "Need some help?"

A male voice, deeper than Matt's, so older.

"Yes, thank you."

"Here you go." I'm up on my feet, but disoriented. Which way is up? Where are Crackers and Beverly?

"Are you okay?"

"I think so. I'm just…I can't…do you see…?"

"Hold on. What can I do for you?"

His voice is full of kindness. He's taller than me, and must have blond hair and blue eyes because he reminds me of the boy I had a crush on in the old neighborhood, David Jaskot.

"I'm with some friends. I'm not sure where they went."

Beverly's voice arrives on the scene. "That was crazy! Want to go again?"

I turn toward the boy who helped me up. "Thanks for helping me. Here's my friend now."

"What's your name?" he asks.

"I'm Hattie."

"I'm Chris Thomas. You live around here?"

"Not really. I live near Puritan and Six Mile. You?"

"Near Grand River and Greenfield. I go to St. Mary's. What about you?"

"We go to Crary," I say. "But I was supposed to go to St. Mary's. My brothers go, but they're younger. What grade are you in?"

"Sixth."

"I'm in fifth."

"Maybe I'll see you around. Maybe at church or something."

"I hope so," I say before I realize.

Crackers drags me away and calls over her shoulder. "Thanks for helping our friend. She's kind of a klutz sometimes!"

"Gee whiz, why didn't you let me talk to him?"

Crackers clucks. "Just what you need. A boyfriend."

Beverly wraps an arm around my shoulder and leads me back up the hill, dragging the sled with her other hand. "This is so cool. You went to the park and met a boy."

"I knew you'd understand," I tell Beverly before I turn to Crackers and make a face.

"Isn't that groovy. You two are boy crazy."

"You're just jealous." Beverly juts out her jaw, or at least that's what I'm guessing. She does that when she's feeling feisty.

Mr. McCracken calls out as we near the top of the hill. "Wish I had a camera with me. You girls are sledding acrobats!"

On the next run, we decide to sit in a circle on the saucer, facing each other, so none of us can see down the hill. On the following run, Beverly and I sit on the sled, and Crackers kneels behind us.

Before too long, we draw an audience. Kids cheer us on

and we conjure up fancier tricks to try. One thing about being blind, I'm fearless. I should be scared about not seeing, but I feel so free soaring down the hill, I don't care.

The next run, Beverly and I kneel, and Crackers stands behind us, holding onto my shoulders. Turns out, Beverly is a great driver.

When we reach the top of the hill again, a hand taps my shoulder.

"Feel like taking a run with me?"

Chris.

"I'm here with my friends. I'd better not."

Beverly gives me a shove from behind. "Go ahead. We'll catch up with you in a bit."

My nerves start to jangle. I want to tell Chris I'm blind. Nobody wants a blind girlfriend, but I would think he already noticed. I'm not wearing sunglasses or anything, so he should be able to tell by seeing my eyes.

"C'mon, let's go."

He's holding my hand and we are walking away from my friends. I'm scared now, in a new way, one I've never felt before, but it's a tingling fear.

CHAPTER TWENTY-TWO

S UNDAY NIGHT, I DREAM MY OWN CINDERELLA FAIRY tale. Chris, my handsome prince, arrives in a gilded carriage, replete with footmen and Clydesdales, ornate jeweled crowns atop their heads. My dress, flowing pale blue taffeta with a full-skirt, twirls and blossoms with each step. I slide on my glass slippers, touch up the blush adorning my cheeks, and toss golden curls from my shoulders.

Cherish plays on my clock radio in the background as my fairy godmother sprinkles stardust in my hair and I wait for my beloved Chris to notice me.

His electric blue eyes glimmer in the moonlight, his smile lighting up his face as he catches sight of me. He takes my hand, and we ride to the ball, the clip-clopping of horse hooves the only sound in the night. Midnight passes without a hitch. I've landed my own Prince Charming.

Mom will have a cow if she discovers I've held hands with a boy, much less dreamt of kissing him. After the Beverly and

Matt incident, the dating scene is years away. At least she can't know my dreams.

I make a mental note to ask Matt if he knows Chris. Maybe through basketball or something.

I gobble my oatmeal with a huge gob of brown sugar, and head out to school in a flurry. Losing myself in my dream put me behind schedule. I'd made the trek to school twice now, me and my trusty cane, there and back, and sometimes I met kids along the way. We'd talk and before I knew it, I'd arrived in one piece.

But this morning, Maxine's voice is the first one I hear as I head down Puritan Avenue.

"Hattie, can I give you a hand?"

Maxine's bad news. She teased me endlessly earlier in the year about wearing glasses and she is the most prejudiced girl in the class—she takes pride in ridiculing Beverly and me because we're friends. She is also the girl who beat up Beverly and me that fateful day in December, and pushed me clear off the swing in the schoolyard.

My insides jumble up, and my chest tightens. "No thanks, Maxine. I've got it."

"Too bad you're blind now."

A lump fills my throat and a burning anger makes my arms tingle with blue flames. *Thanks to you,* I want to scream, but something stands in my way. Still being afraid of her. Worrying I'll start to cry. The thought of not being able to stop being mad if I let even one little ounce of fury escape.

My mind shoots back to Mom's words. "Ignore bullies," and to the saying *sticks and stones can break my bones, but words can never hurt me.* The saying isn't true, but chanting the words over and over again in my head helps.

The WALK sign at the stoplight clicks, and I listen for traffic. If I hurry across the street, I'll be on school grounds. Safer. More kids there. I can call out to a friend. I say a silent prayer. *Crackers. Be there. Beverly. Be there.*

My cane sweeps back and forth in front of me, and I think about using it as a weapon if Maxine comes any closer.

The bell rings, announcing the start of the school day. Nothing has ever sounded so good.

When I reach the top of the stairs a minute later, out of breath and teeth chattering, kids' chitchat echoes around me. If there are so many kids near me, why do I feel so alone?

"Beverly!" I call out. "Crackers!" I spin in circles, like I'm lost in a maze.

"Hey there, Sugar Plum. Big day for me, you know. I'm trying out for the boys' team today."

My heart returns to my chest when I hear her voice. "The boys' team? They'll never let you in the locker room."

"Locker room, schmocker room. I don't need a stinking locker room. I'm the best player in the school. Everybody knows that!"

"Hey, I've got an idea. This can be the next Dream Girls project, the first girl to be allowed on a boys' team."

"Perfect, Hattie. You and your Dream Girls' ideas."

"I'll remind you our last project worked. Kids in our class treat Beverly like a friend now, not like a second-class citizen."

"You're right. They do. For the most part, anyway."

"What's wrong with the Dream Girls having a reputation for breaking barriers, for helping people change their old-fashioned ideas? My mom loves Beverly now, and we don't have to worry about Mrs. Simmons mistreating her. What if you could be the first woman in the NBA? That would be so cool! But we have to start now, because change takes a long time."

Crackers throws her arms around me and squeezes the air right out of me. "Hattie! You're back!"

A smile grows across my face. "You're right," I whisper. "I am."

Just like a speck of dust, my worries about Maxine float away.

"What are you thinking? I see the wheels spinning!"

"I'm making posters, writing a speech, and wondering who I can write a letter to. Maybe Dave Bing or Dave DeBusschere."

"You're the best friend ever!" Crackers slaps me on the back and knocks me into someone.

"Hey, watch out!" Beverly's voice shoots over my shoulder.

"Sorry," I say.

"Oh, it's you, Hattie. No problem."

"Crackers is a little excited today. Basketball tryouts. And…she's trying out for the boys' team."

"Of course she is." Beverly's smile carries in her words. "I'm so proud of her."

"Are you willing to help me write a letter to one of the Pistons? I think if she had their recommendation, the coach might make an exception."

"Hattie's back! Hattie's back!" Beverly sings.

"Just what I said," Crackers shouts. "Let's do it, Dream Girls!"

I can barely concentrate on my classwork and even when I go to Miss Tyler's room to work on Braille, I'm lost in my thoughts.

"Hattie, what's going on today? You seem distracted."

"Sorry, Miss Tyler. My friend is trying out for the basketball team today, and I need to write a letter to one of the Detroit Pistons. I'm going over the letter in my head. If someone from the team saw her play..."

"Her?"

"Yes, Crackers. She plays with the boys at recess and she's better than any of them at dribbling, passing, shooting—she's the best in the entire school. She wants to play with the boys, not on the girls' team. With the boys, she'll be challenging herself, and Crackers is all about a challenge in whatever she does. Whether it's sports, or impressing someone, or changing their mind about her."

"She sounds like an impressive young lady."

"She's fearless. I love her. She's smart and sassy and oh so athletic. She can do whatever she sets her mind to do. I know that for a fact."

"Being allowed to play on the boys' team is not going to happen. Not for years to come, but I admire her for wanting to push herself to such an extreme. Sounds like she might be ahead of her time."

"All the Dream Girls are ahead of their time."

"The Dream Girls?"

"We set up a club a few months ago. Just Crackers and Beverly and me. We made our class understand how to treat everyone the same, regardless of their skin color, or religion, or how smart they are, or how they look."

"Mrs. Simmons told me about your project before I met you. You're an inspiration."

"We all are. We aren't about following the crowd. None of us. We're about making people think, about doing things differently, and about making the world a better place. Martin Luther King, Jr. wrote me a letter. I believe in equal rights. And Crackers being able to play with the boys is about equal rights. She shouldn't be treated differently because she's a girl. Considering her talent, she should be captain of the team, because she's the best."

"That's quite a tall order."

"When Beverly and I first became friends, my mom didn't understand why I wanted to be friends with a black girl. But now, she does. She needed time to know Beverly and see that skin color isn't the way to pick a friend. Maybe the basketball coach will see how talented Crackers is and won't even worry about her being a girl."

"But her gender will affect how the other kids feel, how the parents feel, how the other teams and their coaches will feel."

"It wouldn't be fair not to let her play on the team because she's a girl."

"I hear you," Miss Tyler says, "and if anyone can change old notions, I'm sure the Dream Girls will figure out a way. What can I do to help?"

"Beverly showed me how to write on paper even though I can't see. I use a ruler to keep track of what line I'm on, then I feel the imprint I make on the paper with my pencil to make sure I stay on track. I wrote a story and she looked over my writing, and said I did great. When I'm older, I'm going to invent ways for kids who were previously sighted to do the same thing. Maybe, if I learn science, I can figure a way for blind kids to have a machine which will read to them."

"We already have talking books."

"Those are just recordings though. I'm talking about a device that can read to you, like if you take out a soup can from the cupboard, the tool can read the label for you."

"You're having some very fancy ideas today, Hattie."

I smile and peer in her direction. "This is one of my best days ever."

I meet up with Crackers and Beverly in the cafeteria. Crackers heads over to the hot food line and Beverly and I skid onto the bench at our usual table. "I know Mom will have a kitten if she hears about Chris, but now I know how you feel about Matt."

"My mom thinks I'm too young to go steady with Matt, but we've decided to wait for each other. We might get married someday." She hugs my arm. "We could be sisters, Hattie. Forever family."

"You and Matt would have the cutest kids. Black girls with freckles are so pretty. Your daughter might be the first famous black model."

"She would be the first interracial model."

"You're right!" I pull out my bologna sandwich and take a bite.

Beverly reaches over and wipes my mouth. "You leaked mustard."

I touch my hand to my lips. "Oops. Thanks."

"If you can marry Matt someday, then Crackers can be the first girl on the boys' team. Why don't we stay after school and watch tryouts? Do you think we'll be allowed?"

"We don't have a way to let our moms know."

"We could stop at the office on our way back from lunch and ask if we can call home."

"Great idea!"

Three hours later, Beverly and I sit on the gym floor, our backs against the cold cement block walls, knees folded into our chests. Kids run wind sprints and their feet pound and shake the floor as they pass us. The coach blows his whistle and calls out directions. Shooting drills. Rebounding drills. Dribbling drills.

"Find a partner and practice some passes. One direct pass, then one with a bounce. Back and forth for five minutes."

His shoes squish past me as he directs Tom to partner up with Joe.

Balls bounce on the court, their sharp beats and the squeaks of shoes reverberating through the gymnasium. The room fills with scent of sweat, sweet and tangy. "Martin Blackstone is partnered with Crackers," Beverly says.

Martin, other than George Harrison, has been my secret crush for a while. He's a sixth grader, like Chris. Guess I go for older men. He's a tall, lanky kid, and was runner-up to me in the essay contest. He has freckles and red hair, a lot like my brother Matt, but he's book smart, not street smart, unlike Matt. He's also a true gentleman, so I wonder how he will play ball with Crackers.

She will do whatever is required to make a shot. Slam a player against the wall, or elbow them out of her way. When they play two on two, will he push back?

When boys play with Crackers at recess, they treat her like one of the gang. Guys don't care about pushing each other around on the court, but in front of the coach, I wonder if they will they let a girl go first, or if they'll back away from her.

I'm starting to understand what Miss Tyler means about people not being ready to see a girl play ball on a boys' team. At least nothing will stop Crackers.

I hear the coach. "What's your name?"

"Crackers, Coach."

"That some kind of nickname?"

"Yes, sir. The only name I answer to."

"Crackers, then. Head to the front of the line. Start us off on some lay ups."

She cut her hair short over the weekend. Pretty good thinking if you ask me. If the coach doesn't know, she might be able to pass for a boy. Even Beverly thinks so. Her moves are smooth, and she's aggressive, not mealy-mousy like me when I play, saying, "I can't. I'm not strong enough." Plus, I throw like a girl. Crackers does none of those things.

"I'm open," she calls. "Here!"

Coach Mulder divides the kids into four groups of five, two teams on each side, playing half-court.

On the whistle, play starts.

"You have to be the announcer," I tell Beverly.

"She's on your left. Just passed the ball to Martin. He's dribbling around the defense. A bounce pass back to Crackers. She's going in for the shot. Head first. Knocked Joe down. He's on the floor. She shoots! She scores!"

"I'm proud of you, Beverly. You know a lot about basketball."

"Thanks to Crackers," she says with a lilt in her voice.

The next thirty minutes pass by in a flash. Crackers scores more points than any of the other players. Coach calls them into a huddle and Beverly and I cup our hands behind our ears so we can eavesdrop.

"Great practice today, men. Tomorrow we'll have another day of drills, some two on two and a pick-up game. I'll be making cuts halfway through practice. The remaining fifteen kids will be cut to twelve. I'll post the team roster on the gymnasium door by Wednesday at noon.

"Go home. Get some rest."

Crackers joins us after retrieving her gym bag and stuffing her ball inside.

"I can't believe you," I say. "You were amazing. And I don't think the coach knows you're a girl."

"I can't decide if I'm happy about that, or not. In one way, he should know I'm a girl and be impressed. In another way, I don't want him to know. If he knows, he might have a reason to kick me out of tryouts."

"No way," Beverly says. "This is about skill, not gender."

"Gender, fender," Crackers says. "I'm starved. Let's get some chow."

I have no idea where she thinks we're going to find food, but we head outside and wait for Beverly's dad. He's picking us up when his shift ends, and taking us to their house for dinner. Beverly and I huddle together for warmth. Crackers is still sweaty from running and dances around because she's hyped.

As soon as we go to jump in the cruiser, Crackers pipes up.

"Officer Nichols, may I please sit in the front seat with you?"

A crisscross divider runs across the rear of the front seat, and Beverly and I sit in the back, pretending we were arrested for stealing candy from Clem's Party Store. Crackers hops in the front seat.

"Can I turn on the siren? How about the lights? Can we arrest somebody? What about pulling someone over for speeding? I'd like to write them a ticket. Speeding causes a danger to other drivers as well as pedestrians. Can I read them their rights?"

Officer Nichols' soft chuckle fills the cab, a grunt of disbelief riding on its heels.

"Crackers, when you're old enough to attend the police academy, give me a call. I'll let you ride with me for a day, and you can see some real life criminals first hand. Until then, you can push this button to turn on the flashing lights, and press this one to sound the sirens."

We ride the next two blocks with lights blazing and sirens blaring. At the first corner, Officer Nichols steps on the gas as he turns. So much so that Beverly and I wind up on top of each other, giggling like hyenas at the zoo.

Crackers shrieks from the front seat, "Go get 'em, copper!"

I've only been to Beverly's once, but her house has a special place in my memory. Not just because of the décor, which is like a Victorian storybook, all doilies and brocade upholstery and bookshelves, but because of the smells. Last time we were here, Mrs. Nichols made sweet potato pie and gave us each a lucky penny, which I remembered to slip into my skirt pocket this morning before school. I rub it now, knowing that this is a lucky day because I'm here. The house smells of fried chicken, and Beverly said her mom is making collard greens and okra too. I'm not a fan of unfamiliar foods, but when I tried sweet potato pie, it worked out.

Crackers, on the other hand, loves food, so she's all about it.

"Hey, Mrs. Nichols, I hear we're having black people food tonight."

I want to shush Crackers, she's so brazen, but Mrs. Nichols takes her in stride. "Yes, dear, we're having soul food, so you can see how the other half lives."

Mrs. Nichols surprises me, although she shouldn't. Beverly has the same spunk about her.

"So black people do eat different food. I thought so." Crackers claps her hands and hoots as if she's at the circus. I'd like to throttle her right now.

Beverly, her sweet little self, intervenes. "Crackers, there's something I want to show you in my bedroom. Come here."

I stay in the kitchen with Mrs. Nichols. It's warm and cozy and I'm wondering so many things as I sit there. I work up my courage to ask her something.

"How do you deal with prejudice?"

"What do you mean, Hattie?"

"Well, when Mrs. Simmons was so cruel to Beverly, you told her to forgive Mrs. Simmons because she'd been raised to be prejudiced. And just now, when Crackers was being so crazy about food, you were kind to her. It seems to me like you run into bigotry everyday. Doesn't it make you mad?"

Mrs. Nichols clangs her spoon on the side of a pan, and sets it down. She takes a seat across the table from me and rests her hand atop of mine. "Hattie, the world is a cruel place, you've discovered that already. People probably treat you differently because of your eye difficulties."

"Sometimes they shout at me, like I'm deaf as well as blind. Or they whisper about me, like I can't hear. It's so weird.

"And frankly, I don't understand why skin color or blindness matter. We're all the same on the inside."

Mrs. Nichols takes a deep breath. "We are all the same on the inside. But so many people are threatened by that idea. Some blacks stand up and shout, 'You're treating me different', then they act horribly thinking that striking out is the answer, but they're actually justifying why they are treated differently.

They act like substandard citizens, so they're treated as such."

"I don't want anyone to be treated differently."

"Then you have to act with respect at all times. Respect yourself, and others will respect you."

I tip my head back and close my eyes, thinking about how powerful those words are. "It sounds so simple."

"Sometimes we make life far more complicated than it needs to be."

I bite my lip. This is an important lesson I can't forget.

Crackers comes bursting into the room, "Beverly got a baseball mitt for Christmas!"

I'm as puzzled as I can be. "Are you joking?"

Crackers slaps me on the back. "I'm not. I think her dad thinks I'm a good influence."

Now, that's just hilarious.

CHAPTER TWENTY-THREE

IN THE QUIET OF MY ROOM, I LAY OUT MY PAPER AND PEN. My vision teacher found an address for Happy Hairston, a forward for the Detroit Pistons, who seems totally appropriate for Crackers' mentor, just from his name alone. Plus, Crackers lives for the Pistons. Miss Tyler also offered to read and edit my letter.

February 6, 1968

Dear Mr. Hairston,

I write this letter because I have a very talented friend who plays basketball. You are one of her heroes and I'd like to ask for your help. Crackers is one of the most athletic girls you'll ever meet, and she is trying out for the basketball team at our school. She is one of a kind, spunky as well as talented. I know you would love her.

I'm concerned because girls aren't expected to try out for boys' teams. If you would put in a good word for her, it sure would impress the coach.

I know it's a lot to ask. You might not agree with me, but I think everyone should be treated the same regardless of their skin color or gender.

Thank you for reading my letter and taking time to consider my request.

Sincerely,
Hattie Percha

I cross my fingers after I finish writing, and say a little prayer. My heart catches in my chest. What if Coach Mulder never figures out Crackers is a girl? Could she really pull off tricking him into thinking she's a boy? Not like she's trying to trick him. This is a sin of omission, leaving something out rather than telling.

If I were Crackers, what would I do?

Sometimes, I pretend I'm not blind. Like the day I met Chris at Rouge Park. I didn't tell him I couldn't see. Never mentioned a word. But he had to know. My eyes can't look right anymore.

A funny thing happens lately. There are times I forget I'm blind. I move through the days without thinking about my eyes and the fact I can't see. Maybe I should be happy I forget. Maybe I should be sad. Crackers feels the same way about being a girl trying out for the team. She's both happy and sad to be a girl. Beverly is both happy and sad to be black.

Mom told me a long time ago about being conflicted, when you feel two different ways at the same time. Seems like this is one of those moments. Bittersweet might be a good word too.

I tuck the letter under my bed, being careful to fold down the right hand corner so I remember which paper I need when the time comes to send my message to Mr. Hairston. Waiting for a few days might be best. Maybe Crackers won't need Happy Hairston's help at all.

I'm dreaming again. My rib cage traps my heart. In real life things don't always go according to plan.

Wednesday morning we're all fidgety. Crackers scored double the points of the other players at tryouts yesterday, and she made some impressive passes. She can't stop chattering this morning.

"Guess what, Hattie? Today marks a very special day. I'm going to be the first girl on the boys' team in our school. I bet in all of Detroit. Maybe in all of Michigan. Maybe in the entire United States of America!"

A part of me quakes with excitement for her. Another part is scared silly. If Crackers doesn't make the team because she's a girl, she'll be devastated. Dad says, "Life isn't fair. Get used to it."

When he says this, my blood simmers, rising to a full boil.

Accepting life has its advantages. The serenity prayer tells me to accept the things I can't change. I don't like this part of the prayer. Only a few things are engraved in stone. The weather. Your age. Your gender.

But you can change everything else. With courage, like Martin Luther King, Jr. Like Einstein. Like Abraham Lincoln. I want to be one of those people who believes in change, not settles for bad breaks.

Acceptance has a place in life, more like having a good attitude when things go wrong, but changing things means new possibilities. For kids like Crackers who have talent to be recognized. For Beverly who wants to have a white husband someday. For me who wants people to see who I am, instead of think of me as the blind girl. We all want to be seen the same as everyone else, regardless of our differences.

A fire burns in my belly. My life will make a difference in the world. I may not wind up being a famous trailblazer, but I sure will try.

When the bell announces lunchtime, we rush to the lockers. Beverly and I grab our lunch sacks and meet up with Crackers. The air jumps around her like fleas on a dirty dog. I sense anticipation down to my toes. "What first? Eat or check the gymnasium door?"

"What do you think?" Crackers voice carries a sarcastic edge. "Why put off the best thing to happen in my entire life?"

"I hate to ask you to walk slow, but if I stumble down the stairs, we won't make the trip any faster."

I grasp Crackers hand and squeeze. *Please let her name be on the roster. Please let her name be on the roster.*

We stand in front of the gym door, and I'm trying my darndest to stand still.

"Are you on the team? Where's your name? I want to feel your name on the paper."

"Here's it is! Right here!"

Crackers leaps into the air, waving her arms in the air like a victory flag at the Olympics. "I made the team!"

Beverly and I wrap our arms around her and we jump like pogo sticks.

"This is the best news ever!"

"The world is a good place," Beverly says. "See, Hattie? We did make a difference. Even Coach Mulder doesn't care about whether girls or boys are on the team. Now, you have to write Dr. King and share our victory. The Dream Girls have succeeded again. We've changed the world."

We didn't do anything to change the world this time. Crackers' talent just received the recognition it deserved.

"When is the first game?" I ask.

"I have practice every day after school. I'll let you know as soon as I have a schedule. You'll be there, right? At every game? Cheering me on? This is a gas, baby, can you dig it?"

"I can dig it!" Beverly and I chant in unison. "We can dig it!"

Sorry, Happy. We didn't need your help after all.

CHAPTER TWENTY-FOUR

T HE NEXT DAY, AS SOON AS THE MORNING BELL SOUNDS, Mrs. Foster, the principal, calls our classroom on the P.A. "Mrs. Simmons? Would you please send Ann McCracken to the office?"

Our hearts stop. What could Crackers have done to be called down to the office before school even starts? We turn toward her and the class lets out a collective moan, then a slurry of, "What did you do now?" and "Oh-oh, Crackers is in trouble."

"Pipe down, class. Take your seats. Miss McCracken, you heard Mrs. Foster. Head down to the office and we will see you when you return," Mrs. Simmons says.

Crackers struts past my desk and whispers, "Don't worry your pretty little head. I didn't do anything wrong."

I believe her. At the beginning of the year, Crackers always caused a ruckus, but Mrs. Simmons kept her cool and never sent Crackers to the office, even though a Catholic schoolteacher, especially a nun, would have kicked her out of class for acting so crazy. Maybe Crackers has a message from home or something. Kids sometimes get called to the office for those things, or if they forgot their lunch or homework and their parents dropped it off.

I want to believe this is the case. I really do. But there's this twisting in my gut that tells me there's a problem. I lean across the aisle and whisper to Beverly, "Do you think everything is okay?"

"Don't worry. Crackers can take care of herself."

She has a point.

I tap my foot. Seems like an eternity for Crackers to come back to class.

"Hattie?" Mrs. Simmons says. "Take out your social studies book and follow along."

"You don't get breaks for being blind," Tommy says.

Maxine laughs and my face sizzles as a flush rises up my neck. *Respect yourself.* I repeat the mantra ten times and take a deep breath.

My Braille textbooks weigh a ton, and my social studies book is the heaviest of them all. At least I easily know which book to grab. We are learning about Native American tribes and my mind drifts. They were the first Americans to be discriminated against. We stole their land and killed their animals when we should have treated them with respect. Times like this, I'm not so proud to be white.

I start writing a story in my head about a white girl who goes to live with a Cherokee girl in the North Carolina wilderness after she becomes separated from her family on their journey to California.

Sarah spotted Dancing Flower in the woods, her bow and arrow poised on a rabbit, ready to shoot.

"Stop!" Sarah shouted. "What are you doing?"

Startled, Dancing Flower dropped her weapon.

"Who are you? Why do you stop me?"

"You are about to kill an innocent beast!"

Dancing Flower resumed her stance and zoomed in on her target, aiming and striking down the ball of fur in one swift movement.

"Hattie? Are you with us?"

Oh boy, I'm distracted again. "Sorry."

The door opens and Crackers comes inside. Her shoes with their telltale shuffle make a new sound, one I've heard before, but not in a long, long time. She's stomping mad.

As she thumps by my desk, I reach out and touch her arm. "What's wrong? What happened?"

"Tell you later," are the only words she utters.

The good thing is she's mad and not sad. The bad thing is she's mad.

Crackers doesn't get mad often, and only for a very good reason. But when she's fuming, she usually spouts off, and lets the person she's irate with know all the details. She's seldom quiet.

If Beverly or I are livid, we're more likely to hide our feelings. We stay quiet. Simmer from the inside out.

"What time is it?" I ask my neighbor.

"Five after nine."

The day has just begun. An hour or more until recess. Now I really can't concentrate. Poor Crackers.

I don't hear any of the morning lessons—my head is so full of worries. Time drags, and even when writing class comes, I can't concentrate. My pen sits in my hand like a limp leaf, half-dead.

"Time for recess," Mrs. Simmons announces.

We're out of our seats in a flash, and our teacher says, "Let's try that again, class. Take your seats and I'll dismiss you by rows."

We groan, but do as she asks.

When we reach the hallway, I call for Beverly. "Where are you?"

"Right here. Hurry up. Crackers raced out ahead of us."

"I wonder what happened."

"I have no idea, but she seems fine now. Didn't you notice how she joked around during math class?"

"But she jokes when she's sad. Or when she's mad."

"Or when she's happy," Beverly reminds me. "Plus, she ran outside like the building is on fire."

"I still want to check on her."

"Crackers is right about you, Hattie. You're a worrywart."

I laugh. "I was born this way."

When we reach the playground, Crackers is playing football with the boys. It's freezing out here and the wind whips my hair in my face. The air is heavy with moisture, a warning, more snow is about to fall. After the fresh dusting we received last night, we're in for a good six inches. Dad said so this morning.

"Want to do the monkey bars?" Beverly asks.

"Sure, as long as Maxine isn't over there."

"Well, she is. You have to give her another chance. I know you don't like her, but maybe if you think about her differently, you'll learn to like her."

"I don't know how you can be so nice to someone so hateful. Maxine has an ugly mouth and I don't trust her for a minute." I scowl whenever I think about trying to be nice to Maxine.

"She's not too bad," Beverly says.

"Tell me one nice thing about her."

A long silence later, Beverly says, "All right. You've made your point."

Someone taps my shoulder, and I turn. "Crackers?"

"Yep, Dipstick. It's me."

"What's wrong?" She calls me names, but silly ones, not mean ones.

"Coach Mulder figured out I'm a girl. When he posted the roster, he wrote Crackers McCracken. When Tommy's dad heard I made the team and he didn't, he called Mrs. Foster to complain."

"That's so unfair."

"I'm not giving up. I'm going to practice today. Tommy can't shoot a hoop for beans. He shouldn't be on the team."

"Maybe the coach will fight for you. He likes you, I can tell."

"No worries, Hattie. I've foiled the best-laid plans of adults before—I'm not about to stop now. They haven't seen the last of Crackers."

I snatch Beverly's coat sleeve. "Do you have a pen and paper?"

Beverly reaches inside her pocket. "Always!"

"Let's start a petition right now." I start to dictate.

"Crackers has been dismissed from the Crary basketball team because she's a girl. If you believe she should be allowed to play for our school, please sign below."

"Got it, Hattie."

"Give me the paper. I'll get signatures."

I make my way around the playground with Beverly by my side. We talk to kids and pass the notebook back and forth. Everyone wants to sign. Beverly ends up starting a second sheet.

The entire time I'm gathering signatures my mind is swirling like a spinning top. I don't even notice that my fingers have turned to icicles. We need Mr. Hairston's help after all. He's a black man, so he must understand discrimination. I bet he's worn Beverly's shoes and been ridiculed for being black. If he sees Crackers play, he can help us.

At the end of recess, we have fifty-two signatures. Tommy huddles with his friends Brian, Tim, John, and Jim. I can eavesdrop if I listen very close. Tommy wants to start a campaign against Crackers, but he doesn't have paper to collect signatures saying girls shouldn't be allowed.

Brian pipes up. "Let's put up posters like when we vote for student council. No girls allowed."

Boys. Stupid boys.

I wonder how Mrs. Foster really feels. She seems like a fair principal. But I know Dad says adults have to take orders too. Maybe she had no choice but to ban Crackers from the team. I make a mental note to talk to her. She likes the Dream Girls. If she knows we were about to change Crary School again, maybe she'll support us.

Crackers slaps me on the back when Mrs. Simmons blows the whistle.

"Hattie, Hattie, go to battie," she recites. "You're the best friend a girl could ever have. You too, Bev Jo. I bet my mom is smiling up in heaven right now."

CHAPTER TWENTY-FIVE

FUNNY HOW SOUND I SLEPT. AFTER I POLISHED THE letter to Happy Hairston, I wasn't tired at all. And the thought of getting enough signatures on our petition to make a difference is beyond anything I ever dreamed. The weird part is, my fingers jiggled with adrenalin. This is the most important thing I've ever done next to the experiment the Dream Girls did with our class. The Civil Rights Movement happened at just the right time.

"You're destined for great things, Hattie." Dad says that to me sometimes. I hope they're right. I want to do great things. I want to leave a mark on the world.

While I'm eating breakfast I ask Mom, "Can I have Crackers and Beverly over for a Dream Girls meeting Saturday?"

"Hold on a minute," she says. "I have to check the calendar." She drops Larry in my lap and strides over to the wall calendar next to the phone. "What time?"

I share some of my cereal with my baby brother and he

makes happy sounds.

"Can I check with them at school today? If you want, I could tell them a time."

"Let's say lunchtime. You can meet in the basement after."

"Thanks! You're the best! I think we can convince the school to let Crackers play on the team."

"If not this year, Hattie, maybe next."

"Don't say that! She has to play this year. She has to!"

"Don't count your chickens."

"Mom, you have to have faith in me. You have to have faith in the dream."

Mom lets out a soft chuckle. I know she's proud of me.

"Off to school you go. If you don't leave now, you'll be late."

The air is mild today and the sun warms my face as I walk down the street. The weatherman was wrong about the snow.

"Hi, Hattie. Do you need some help?"

"No thanks, Maxine. What's up? Nice day, huh?"

"The sun feels good, but I hate being cold."

"I like the cold mostly."

"You're doing a great job, Hattie. Being blind, I mean."

"Everybody has something they have to deal with." Now seems like a good time to use Grandma's words.

"My mom has trouble hearing, but she's mad about it. She yells at us all the time. You don't seem mad."

"I am sometimes, but I tell myself my eyes will heal. Being blind won't last forever."

"You're really good with the cane. And I saw the contraption you use to make those dots on your paper."

"A stylus. And the dots are called Braille."

"Braille looks like fun. Is it hard to learn?"

"No, it's cool really, the way the dots stand for words and letters."

"You know more than one language!" Maxine grabs my arm. "Watch out, there's a patch of ice in your path. Here, take my arm, I'll lead you around it."

We negotiate the ice and find smooth sidewalk, clear of snow.

"Maxine," I say, taking a moment to straighten my shoulders.

"What?"

We stop in the middle of the sidewalk and I turn to face her. Even though I can't see, I want her to know I'm willing to stand up to her. That I'm not afraid of her anymore.

"I've been really angry with you for a while now. I have a problem with anger. It makes me uneasy, so I clam up. But the fact is, you're a part of the reason I'm blind. I've tried forgiving you, because I know it's the right thing to do, but I can't trust you or be your friend. I'd like to forgive you. I really would, but you are nice one minute and hateful the next. You need to take responsibility for your actions. You need to say you're sorry."

"One of the reasons people don't like you is because you're preachy. That's how we can tell you're Catholic. You act like you know more than everybody else. You act like you're better than everybody else."

Her words flatten me, like I was just run over by a bulldozer. My shoulders slump. "I never knew that."

"Well, it's true."

"Then I guess I should thank you for letting me know. Still, what about the fact that you pushed me down? What about the fact that you and your friends beating me up caused me to be blind? Is this your excuse?"

"Maybe."

Now it's Maxine's turn to think.

"I feel really guilty about your eyes, Hattie. I lie in bed at night and think about it. I never meant for this to happen, and if I could, I'd take it back right this minute, so you could see again."

"It's not that easy."

"I know. Honest, I do. Is there a way for me to make it up to you?"

"What, like be my personal servant for the rest of my life?" I'm not sure where that came from, but now that I let myself get mad, I can't seem to turn it off.

"Hattie, I really am sorry. Could you just try to trust me?"

"I'm not sure. I'll have to think about it."

"Fair enough."

We turn and start walking again, both of us quiet, just listening to the hum of traffic on the pavement.

A few seconds later, Maxine speaks up. "Maybe you could teach our class a lesson. Lots of kids would like to try out your cane too."

"When we get to school, I can show you. I'm allowed to go inside before the bell. Want to?"

When Crackers and Beverly come up to the lockers, their voices interrupt Maxine and me. "Hey, Hattie! What's up?"

Maxine has my cane and she's tapping back and forth between the classroom and her locker. Her eyes are supposed to be closed, but Crackers gives me the lowdown.

"Maxi," she says. "Let's blindfold you. No peeking."

Before long, a line of kids forms, all waiting for Crackers to wrap a scarf around their eyes and take a turn with the cane. I stand at the front, popping out directions.

"When it's your turn, hold the cane in the center of your body and point it down at a forty-five degree angle. See how Maxine is holding it?" I take hold of the cane and help her swing it in an arc, keeping her hand in the center of her body. "The tricky part is coordinating your steps with the cane. Tap, step, tap, step."

Mrs. Simmons voice enters the hallway. "What do we have here?"

"Hattie is teaching us how to see with a cane!" Crackers announces. "We all want to have a chance to try. Please, Mrs. Simmons! This is way more important than reading!"

"Only if I can be next."

The entire hall erupts in applause. "Go, Mrs. Simmons, go!"

My heart swells like a balloon. Today is a day of second chances.

"Here, Mrs. Simmons," Maxine says as she hands our teacher my cane and Crackers sidles up behind her.

"Lean down," Crackers says, "and tell me if you can see under the scarf. No cheating."

"Cheater teacher, wouldn't wanna be her."

Crackers elbows me, and in turn, I slug Beverly in the side. Mrs. Simmons just made a joke. She totally sounded like Crackers.

When Crackers' turn comes around, she wields the cane, swishing the stick through the air like a sword. "On guard," she says, and the entire class giggles.

Beverly's turn comes last. "The important thing to remember," she says, "there is more than one way to do things. Hattie walks using a cane, I trip over things even though I use my eyes, and Crackers, well, Crackers flies though the air like a trapeze artist!"

Mrs. Simmons calls the class to order and asks us to join her inside the room to start the day. "Whose idea was this?"

I raise my hand. "Maxine's!"

"Nice idea, Maxine."

"I want Hattie to teach us Braille too." There is a lilt to Maxine's voice I haven't noticed before.

"What a fine suggestion! But we have work to do. Perhaps another day."

I kind of like Maxine. It's surprising, but maybe, just maybe I can be friends with her after all.

I lean over to Crackers. "How did practice go last night?"

"Coach let me practice, but he says he can't let me back on the team."

"What did your dad say?"

"He's hopping mad, but he's not sure there's anything to be done."

"Don't be so sure," I whisper across the aisle. "Dream Girls' meeting, my house. Saturday. Noon."

Mrs. Simmons taps her pencil on the desk. "Reading books, ladies. Join us now, please."

Beverly and I leave class first for recess. As we mosey down the steps, she says, "I'm so proud of you, Hattie. You and Maxine looked like you were having fun this morning."

"I decided to give her a final chance. You're so nice to everyone, even after they hurt you."

"Mom taught me a lot about forgiveness," Beverly says as she rubs my arm. "Staying mad and holding grudges is a choice. Anger takes more energy than forgiveness. Offering forgiveness is like giving a gift."

"I'll have to think about that one. Deep thinking, Beverly. Way deep."

"Think about how bad you feel when you've hurt someone's feelings. Even one of your brothers."

"You're right. I feel guilty, but I don't have an easy time admitting when I make a mistake. You're better at confessing than me. I keep secrets about my screw-ups. I try to hide my faults."

"You're really strong. What's best about being friends with you and Crackers is how we all bring out the best in each other. I love you so much, Hattie!" Beverly's voice quivers with emotion.

"One thing I know for sure, nothing will ever stop us. No matter what happens."

"Big dreams for Dream Girls." Beverly's voice lights up the room.

Crackers runs up behind us, tossing her arms around us in a giant hug. "This is another good day! Remember how we used to play Bad Thing, Good Thing? Now we only talk about good things."

"We should still talk about both," Beverly says.

"We used to tell each other secrets too. We should do that again," I say as we step outside into the cold, still air.

"Can I go first?" Crackers asks.

Beverly and I laugh. What else is new? "What?" We say in unison.

"It's not a bad thing, but it's deep. Like really deep."

"Don't keep us in suspense."

Crackers voice goes sad and low. "Dad told me last night he thinks my mom would be proud of me for being a good student and for having such great friends. He even got a little teary. Dad never talks about Mom. It made me realize something. He misses her. I miss her. All the time. It's like I've got a hole in my heart."

We wrap our arms around Crackers and hold on tight.

How could she not?

CHAPTER TWENTY-SIX

"WE HAVE TO DO SOMETHING SPECIAL FOR Crackers."

Mom stops stirring the spaghetti sauce. "Why?"

"She misses her mom." I crumple with the words, tears blanketing my cheeks.

The spoon bangs on the side of the pot, and soon Mom's arms encircle my shoulders. "Oh, dear. The poor thing."

"How can anyone live without a mom?"

"I'm not sure, but Crackers is such a resilient girl, she'll be all right."

"Still, we should do something."

"Why don't we have her stay for dinner Saturday after the Dream Girls' meeting? If you like, invite her to spend the night. We can play family games after dinner. I bet time with us will help."

"She has a hole in her heart, Mom."

"We all have holes in our hearts. This is Crackers' hole. But think about what she's accomplished even without her mom. Some people in her position would be lost and alone all the time, but Crackers is tough. She's learned how to handle her loss."

"By being funny and athletic? Is that what you mean?"

"Yes, she's finding her way. Times will arise when she is sad and lonely, but don't worry. She'll be all right."

"Maybe since she can't be on the boys' team, she misses her mom now more than ever."

"I'm guessing you're exactly right."

"When something bad happens to me, I miss you, even if you're just down here cooking dinner and I'm up in my room."

"Then you need to come right downstairs and find me. And if I'm not close by, think of me. I'm as close as your thoughts."

"Grandma is like a second mom to me." I reach out and touch my hand to Mom's face, tracing her profile with my finger—her strong nose, her high cheekbones, her full lips, her long feathery eyelashes. I remember Mom's face even though I can't see her anymore. I wonder if Crackers remembers her mom's face. "Maybe you could be a second mom to Crackers."

"I can certainly try."

"We have lots of kids in our family, but I've always wanted a sister. Crackers could be my unofficial sister!"

"Does she like desert? I'll make a lemon meringue pie."

"Do you think Beverly will feel left out if we don't invite her?"

"Why don't you explain our plan? She'll understand."

"Great idea, Mom! We should bring the hockey game to the living room. We can take turns. You know, winner plays whoever is next. Like a tournament."

"You better warn Crackers. Dad doesn't let anyone win. He plays fair. If he's better than Crackers, he'll beat her."

"She'll beat him. She and Matt played when we had the overnight. He likes playing with her. All the boys do."

"She'll fit right in at our house."

"Boys galore."

The sauce starts to bubble on the stove, and Mom goes back to stirring the pot. The aroma of oregano and garlic make my mouth water.

Mom's probably glad Beverly isn't staying for dinner. If she did, she'd have to worry about Beverly and Matt sneaking off for a kiss. My eyes smile at the thought.

I look toward the window, a shadow entering my eyes.

"Mom! Mom! I can see the light."

"I see the light, too, Hattie, every now and then."

"No, I'm not talking about an idea popping into my head. I really see light. The sun is coming in through the window. Shadows are dancing on the wall. Can you see them too? Am I just imagining?"

Mom steps over to where I'm sitting and leans down to where I'm looking. She inhales sharply and the room goes still for a solid thirty seconds.

"I see them too, Hattie."

Chills run up my arms. I see something. Just a shadow bobbing around light, but I can see!

"I'll call Doc Baker." She rushes to the phone, flips through the directory and dials. "This is Joan Percha, Hattie's mom. I'd like to schedule an appointment for my daughter. She's seeing some shadows.

"Oh, I see. Yes, I'll call back in the morning." She hangs up the phone and stays quiet.

"What?" I ask. "What's wrong?" My heart sinks to my stomach. Maybe the nurse doesn't believe Mom. Maybe…

"Don't worry, honey. The office is closed for the day, that's all. That was his service for emergencies."

"Isn't this an emergency? Where's a flashlight? I want to see if I can see anything else."

"Tell me what you see."

"I see a shadow on either side of a slice of light. And it's coming from the window, so it's sunlight, right?"

Dad strides into the kitchen, his footsteps hitting heavy on the linoleum. "How are my two favorite girls?"

Mom and I both start speaking at once. Neither one of us can speak a coherent word.

"What's wrong? Did someone get bad news?"

"No! I can see, Dad, I can see!"

Dad's voice travels between Mom and me. "Tell me about this."

"I see light coming through the window. Before everything was always dark, but now I can tell the difference between light and dark. I know! I can go in the closet with a flashlight. Then, I'll really be able to tell if my eyes are working. They're healing. I know they are."

I rub the goosebumps on my arms and Dad opens and closes the junk drawer. Thunk. Thunk. "Here's a flashlight. Go. Try out your idea and see."

"Want to come?"

"I'm not sure both of us can fit in the closet with all those winter coats in there. I'll stand outside the door. Tell me how things go."

His voice is excited, like Thomas Edison discovering the light bulb, but he's trying to stay calm.

Mom trails behind us as we step to the hall. My brothers have caught the buzz in the air. They are all standing at the bottom of the stairs, the war they were fighting with their army men gone quiet.

"Step back, boys. Be very quiet. Hattie needs space and silence."

Dad opens the closet door for me and kicks some shoes aside. "There is a space for you right here. Sit on the floor and I'll shut the door."

"Is Hattie in trouble?" Johnny asks.

"Why are you putting Hattie in the closet?" Rob chuckles and says to Matt, "At least you're not the one in hot water for a change."

Mom scolds them. "I asked you to be quiet."

I huddle on the floor of the closet, inhaling the scent of well-worn shoes, leather and dust. The tiny room is pitch black. I blink several times to be sure. The hard, cold flashlight rests in my hand, and I take a deep breath before I push up the switch, squeezing my eyes shut tight. I direct the light's head toward the back wall and open my eyes. There's a dark orb on the plaster, shady with uneven edges, but around the misshapen blob is a circle of light. Then another circular splotch and more light.

My eyes fill with tears and now I can't see a thing. I wipe my eyes, blink and look again. I think about how Doc Baker examines my eyes, first one, and then the other. I close my left eye and turn on the light. Nothing. I switch eyes and try again. My left eye is the one that is working. But that's a good sign. One of my eyes is healing, the other is sure to follow. Eyes are like that.

"Hattie?" Dad's voice. Then, a soft knock on the door.

"Hattie?" Mom this time.

I want to stay right here, nestled in this closet forever,

crowded and covered with coats and scarves, smelling sweaty feet. I can't speak. Not yet.

"I can see!" I finally let out. "I can see light. Only with my left eye, but still…"

"Can I open the door," Dad jokes, "or are you going to stay in there all night?"

My brothers are whooping in the hallway. "Hattie can see! Hattie can see!"

"Calm down, boys. Give her a minute."

After several long moments, the place goes quiet, just left-over whispers of voices seep through the door.

I turn the light off and on, testing my eyes. I want to see so bad, I have to make sure I'm not imagining. "I want to stay here. Just five more minutes."

Dad directs everyone to the kitchen. "Time to set the table, Rob. Matt, make sure your brothers all wash their hands for dinner."

A herd of feet stomp down the stairs to the back hall landing and into the bathroom. "Come to the kitchen when you're done," Dad calls out after them.

Mom taps on the door and says softly, "Take your time, Hattie. I can't wait to hear all about your eyes." Her voice holds hope.

I kick shoes out of my way and hunch in the back of the closet, flashing the light here and there, checking to make sure I can see the light from various angles, not just in the one spot. I can. I sit there for a long time, the warmth shrouding me like a downy comforter. Safe. Warm. Seeing.

My stomach grumbles. Probably because I smell the pasta boiling and because I didn't have a snack after school. I want to eat, but I hate to leave. This is the first place I ever saw again.

I'll never forget this moment. Curled up in a jumble of coats, leggings, umbrellas, hats, mismatched gloves, sitting with dust bunnies, I saw again for the first time. This is the best day of my life!

I open the door to the closet and hear the murmuring of my eating family, clinking dishes and asking for the Parmesan cheese to be passed around the table. I tiptoe into the bathroom and close the door, pulling down the window shade and sitting on the toilet, turning on the flashlight again and closing my left eye, then trying the same thing with my right eye. This time I can't see the light. Maybe it's still light outside and the sun's rays are leaking around the edges of the shade. Goosebumps rise again, this time all over my body. Even my toes.

I wash my hands under the spray of warm water and stroll into the kitchen, like today is an ordinary day.

The room goes midnight quiet.

"Well?" Matt finally says. "Don't just sit there. We want to know what's going on."

Mom fills my plate and hands it to me. "Spaghetti at ten o'clock, peas at six, garlic toast at eight."

I fill my mouth with a bite of spaghetti, sauce dripping off my chin. "I'm starving. Tell you in a minute."

"She's doing this on purpose, Dad," Rob tattles like he always does. Only this time I haven't done anything wrong.

"I'm really hungry. I'm not being mean. Hold on." I shove a mouthful of garlic bread in my mouth. This is the best meal I've ever tasted.

"My left eye is the one that's working so far. I'm sure my right eye will catch up. I can see a light in the closet when I'm in total darkness, but not in the bathroom with a window. I don't know how I saw the sun coming through the kitchen window, because it wasn't dark then, was it, Mom?"

"No, not yet."

"In the closet, I can see the flashlight."

"What does it look like?" Dad says with his mouth full. He'd yell at us for talking with our mouths full, but he's excited right now and all the rules are out the door.

"Blobby. There's a dark spot and then a ring of light around a smudge, sort of like a halo."

"You can just say 'halo,' Hattie, don't use 'like' all the time." Now Dad's back to acting like a teacher.

"We will see Doc Baker soon, and see what he thinks."

"Will Hattie be able to see everything?" Johnny asks.

"We don't know yet, son," Dad says, "but her eyes appear to be getting better. This is a very good sign. Let's raise our glasses to Hattie."

We lift our glasses and touch them to clink. "Congratulations, Hattie!" Rob says.

"Good going, Hattie," says Matt.

Baby Larry claps his hands.

Yes, Crackers needs a family just like mine.

CHAPTER TWENTY-SEVEN

D OC BAKER SEATS ME IN FRONT OF THE ophthalmoscope and I twirl on the chair. I can't wait to show off my eyes!

The plastic cup of the machine is cold and hard when I rest my chin on top, and the doctor says, "Not so fast, Hattie. Let me put a tissue there for you." He chuckles a deep, throaty laugh, and his fingers guide my face back to the machine.

"Look straight ahead," he says.

I do as I'm told, telling the tightening knots in my stomach not to worry. After a few "ahems" and "aha's", Doc sits back on his stool and pushes across the floor.

Mom rests her hand on my shoulder, but soon her usually tender touch seizes me like a vice grip and I yelp.

"Sorry, honey, I guess I'm as anxious as you are to hear what the doctor has to say."

"As you suspected, this is good news. But let's make it medically official. I confirm your suspicions. Your left eye is healing,

Hattie. Now, we have to play the patience game again. This is a very positive sign, though. There is every chance your vision will be restored to some extent. Unfortunately, I can't give you a date, nor can I tell you it will return with the clarity you once had."

"How about a week from Tuesday? That's my friend's first official basketball game. I want to see her play."

"There is no timeline in these cases. Your vision could come back tomorrow, or could take up to a year. You may be able to determine just light and dark or at some point see shapes and colors. The process is different for each individual, as is the result."

"Will I be able to read and write again?"

"The possibility certainly exists. I wish I had a crystal ball, but I'm afraid it's in the shop."

My shoulders slump. I like things to happen fast. I'm horrible at waiting.

Mom reads my mind because she says, "You've waited this long, Hattie. You can hang in there a bit longer."

I kick my toe at the machine. "I guess."

Mom schedules another appointment for me for two weeks from now and we head to the car. She pats my knee once we're loaded inside. "All good things…"

"Come to those who wait," I finish.

"Want to get ice cream?"

"Before lunch? In the winter?"

"Why not! It's never a bad time for ice cream."

Mom and I stroll into Sanders, swinging our arms like a pendulum. I leave my cane in the car. "Do my eyes look normal?"

"They are as beautiful as always, Hattie, green emeralds in

a stormy sea."

"Why stormy?"

"With all those copper strands around them, they stand out. That's all."

"I thought you meant because I'm sort of disappointed today."

Mom chuckles softly. "That too."

She lets me order whatever I want, even though I'm sure to spoil my lunch. I order a cream puff hot fudge sundae with whipped cream, no cherry, and a lemon coke.

She orders the special, a Pecan Titan sundae with butter pecan ice cream and extra hot fudge.

Reading and math are already over when I get to school. Beverly and Crackers both whisper to me as I stride down the aisle to my desk. "Are you sick? Is everything okay?"

Mrs. Simmons shushes them. "Wait until recess, girls."

Everyone wants a turn to leave class early and walk downstairs with me when the halls are clear. Today is Maxine's turn.

"Why were you late today?"

I don't want to say. The Dream Girls should be the first to hear the news. Plus, I haven't even decided whether or not to tell them. Having people know and bug me about being able to see might be aggravating. Or disappointing if I don't get better fast. Or...

"Hattie?"

"Sorry, Maxine, I was thinking about what I missed this morning. What did you do in math?"

"I'm no good at math. I can't even tell you."

"You're not as bad as you think. Just try. The more you practice, the better you'll be."

"You sound like Mrs. Simmons."

We fall into laughter. "Good one, Maxine."

Crackers charges up behind us. "What's the word, Hattie bird?"

Maxine dashes off to play on the monkey bars, even though her fingers might turn to popsicles today.

Beverly joins us. "Where were you this morning? We were worried you were sick."

"Not sick. Just at a doctor's appointment."

They wait. Just the Dream Girls and me, standing in the frigid air, kids rushing past us, calling for their friends. "You're invited to my house for lunch Saturday, remember? Did you check if you could come?"

"I can!" Beverly titters.

"Me too! Get it. Me two. Me too."

Beverly groans and I shake my head.

I squint in the sun, trying to make out shapes and shadows, hoping for a glint of color to flash before my eyes.

"I can tell the difference between dark and light. Just with my left eye, but I can see some shadows," I blurt out.

Beverly smiles with her voice. "This is the best news. Things are looking better all the time."

"I wonder if we will hear from Happy Hairston soon. I want you to be able to play that first game, Crackers."

"Game, shame," Crackers says. "Dad talked to Coach Mulder last night. He says there's nothing he can do. The rules specifically state you have be a boy to play on the boys' team and a girl to play on the girls' team."

"Play on the girls' team then." I finger the zipper on my jacket, hoping she'll say yes.

"There's no competition there. It would be like playing with babies. I won't improve if I'm not challenged. Even Dad agrees."

"But if you don't play at all, that will be like giving up on your God-given talent," Beverly says. "You can't give up."

"I'm not playing anymore. I'm not giving up, but I'm not conforming to a bunch of stupid rules either."

This might be one of those times when Crackers is being her own worst enemy. Dad says we all do this: stand in our own way because we're stubborn. "I remember when we got in trouble for the fight. Dad told me to stay between the lines to accomplish my goals. Not break rules, but find a way around them. You always find ways around things. You are the one who taught me that. We aren't done yet. Don't give up. Don't give in."

"So what you're saying is we need to look beyond the lines."

"The world has been dark for me for over a month. Now it's fuzzy. Think about this like a metaphor. Beyond the lines might mean…" My head begins to throb. I haven't thought this through yet, but I might be about to make a new discovery.

"Beyond the lines might mean…" I start again, but nothing comes.

"Beyond the lines means we have to find a new way to think about this. Right now, the coach, the parents, and the school thinks the teams have to be made up a certain way. If we can prove them wrong, they might come around." Beverly stops and waits for us to answer her.

My mouth drops open, and Crackers is totally silent. Not herself at all.

"Saturday. Three days away. By Saturday we will think of a solution. Everyone's job is to bring three ideas to the Dream Girls' meeting. Think of five in case any of us have the same idea, then pick your top three ideas and we'll go from there, okay?"

Silence.

"What?" I ask. "What's going on?"

"Sorry, Hattie. We were nodding. We agree," Beverly says.

Saturday weather threatens our Dream Girls' meeting. Snow fell like a thick blanket overnight, a coating of icy frosting on top, and the roads are iffy. It's a good thing no one lives far away. I'm still crossing my fingers and toes though. I want both Beverly and Crackers to come. Beverly understands about Crackers spending the night, and she even agrees. She might have Crackers to her house too. Mrs. Nichols is as great a mom as mine, so if Crackers has both a second and a third mom to make up for hers, she might be better off than the two of us.

I make my bed and fluff up the extra pillow. I hope I don't hog the bed tonight. And I hope Crackers doesn't fling her arms in my face all night like my brother Johnny does when he sleeps with me. For some reason I think she will. She never stops moving.

The doorbell rings at noon. Beverly arrives first and my parents chat with Officer Nichols in the foyer. Dad asks him about work, and he tells Dad a story about working with a white officer who didn't want him as a partner because of his skin color. I'm sad to think of all the prejudice. If only we learned something from the riots and could get along with each other.

My neighbor friend, Colleen, who attends St. Mary's, her house is for sale. Even though it's the dead of winter. No one wants to move in the winter. Not if they have kids. But Colleen's parents don't want to be in Detroit anymore. Poor Colleen. She has to move to a suburb where she doesn't know anyone. I thought about telling her she can come and visit, but I haven't been back to my old neighborhood once in the seven months since we moved, and I've never talked to or written to any of my old friends.

Beverly and I tromp up to my room and then scurry to the basement, ideas in hand, and place them on the coffee table, face down, until our meeting. No peeking ahead of time. It's an unspoken rule of the club.

Crackers arrives ten minutes late, but that's because her dad had trouble shoveling the driveway at their house. It's gravel, not pavement like Beverly's and mine. Mr. McCracken and Dad talk about cars. Dad wants a new station wagon pretty soon, but we've never had a Ford, only a GM, so he's thinking of trying one out.

Crackers bounds down the stairs, kangaroo-style, hopping and making weird noises.

"Put your ideas on the table."

She snatches them out of her bag and slaps them on top of the pile. "What's for lunch? I'm starving."

"She's always hungry," Beverly says as if Crackers isn't standing right there.

"Mom made tuna noodle casserole. A hot lunch."

"I made a casserole one time," Crackers says.

"You did?" The girl freaks me out.

"No. Just kidding."

"Girls! Lunch time!" Mom calls down the stairwell.

"Be right there, Mrs. Percha!" Crackers turns on the charm once again.

Beverly and I hold hands as we follow Crackers to the kitchen. We take our seats and serve ourselves gigantic servings of the rich noodles. Mom puts crisp potato chips on top, so we fight over who will have the crustiest serving.

I smell oatmeal cookies with raisins and walnuts for dessert. With a cold glass of milk, there's nothing better than fresh-baked cookies.

"What a fine lunch, Mrs. Percha," Crackers says. "Thanks for inviting me. What are we having for dinner?"

Beverly and I giggle until we almost wet our pants.

"I'll get back to you on that, dear," Mom says. I know she's baking the pie while we have our meeting.

We deliver our dishes to the sink then hurry downstairs to share our ideas, sitting in a circle on the floor.

"Want me to read yours first, Hattie?"

"Mine are written in Braille, silly. I'll read them. Who wants to go first?"

"Stupid question," Crackers says as she begins to read her list. "My first idea is to change my name to Chuck."

"Be serious," Beverly says. "Tell us a real idea."

"File a formal complaint against the athletic department of Detroit Schools. You guys write it, I'll mail it. Second idea is to hire a lawyer that works in Hattie's grandma's firm. We can claim a violation of the Civil Rights act. Third idea, get Martin Luther King, Jr. involved. He's a friend of Hattie's and I hear he and Mayor Cavanaugh are friends."

Beverly and I ponder Crackers' ideas for a few minutes. None of them seem realistic. "I'll read mine next. Then, your turn, Hattie." She pauses and clears her throat. "First, we could continue to have kids sign our petition. We could also have kids ask their parents to write a letter to Mrs. Foster, the Board of Education, and the athletic department in support of Crackers being on the team. Second, we prepare a presentation for the school board, arguing our points like a debate team—we're smart and articulate—we have great vocabularies. They might listen to us, especially if they hear about our class demonstration and how you won the essay contest, Hattie, and heard from Dr. King. Third, we have an exhibition game. We find kids who are willing to play in the game, good players, who want to play with Crackers, so it's a fair and challenging game. They don't let her show off or anything, but her natural talent shines through. We invite school officials, city officials, the newspapers, teachers, parents, kids… "

"I don't even want to share my ideas, Beverly. This is the best one. I'm sure."

Crackers runs in circles like someone planted a motor inside her.

"Best idea ever! Beverly, you are a genius!"

Not long ago, Beverly and Crackers weren't sure about the Dream Girls. We've come a long way, the three of us.

CHAPTER TWENTY-EIGHT

I BEG MOM TO BORROW HER TYPEWRITER AND TELL BEVERLY how I mastered writing the letter to Happy Hairston with the addresses at the top of the letter with the date and the opening and closing.

"I know, Hattie. Relax."

"I'm excited is all."

"Maybe we're getting ahead of ourselves. We have to check and see where we can hold the game, when, and who will play."

"We don't have much time. The first game of the season is next week."

"The season lasts for a while. Even if Crackers doesn't play in the first game, she can play in another. Think long term, not just today."

"How are you so smart?" Crackers asks.

Beverly purses her lips. I know this without seeing her. Her eyes are probably twinkling too. She's humble, but proud of her intelligence. She's like her mom.

"We need an adult who will listen."

We're quiet for a while. Thinking. Thinking.

"My dad. He works for Detroit Schools. He will know someone. And, he's right upstairs. Hold on. I'll get him."

I race upstairs, tripping over a pile of shoes in the back hall, landing on my butt. I shake the stars from my head and stand, holding onto the rail this time and calling out, "Dad, can you come here?"

"What is it?" he says as he makes his way from the den to the hallway.

"Can you come downstairs? We need some advice about an idea we have."

"Sure thing." Dad tramps down the stairs, trailing behind me. Crackers pulls out a chair for him at the card table. "Thanks for joining us, Mr. Percha."

Dad scrapes his chair across the floor as he pulls himself up to the table. "How can I help?"

"We have a great idea! Beverly's idea, really. You tell him, Bev Jo."

Beverly clears her throat. "As you know, Crackers isn't allowed to play on the boys' basketball team because she's a girl. Our idea is to hold a game and let Crackers demonstrate her talent. If we can convince the right people to come, we might be able to change the minds of the coaches, the people who decide these rules like the Board of Education or the Athletic Department."

"I'm not sure if the Michigan Department of Education has rules about this, but the Michigan High School Athletic Association has gender rules. A team can be disqualified from the league if they have a boy playing on a girls' team or vice versa. There aren't any specific rules at the elementary level. It's more a matter of policy. They haven't faced opposition in the past, but you're up against history. And conservative ideas."

"But this is a good idea, isn't it?"

"A very good idea. Hold on a minute. Let me think."

Crackers springs up from the table, her footsteps falling in perfect rhythm as she paces back and forth.

"We might be able to hold the game at the high school."

"Cody?"

"I can sign out the gym. The schedule is tight this time of year, but we can hold the game off hours. I'll check the calendar."

Beverly pipes up. "Do you know anyone from the news or TV stations?"

"Marilyn Turner has been at the Auto Show when I've played there."

Dad's band plays lots of jobs at local venues. Why didn't I think of this?

"Hattie, your godfather works for the Detroit News. I'll call him and see what he thinks."

"This is perfect, Dad!"

"Hold your horses, I said I'll try. I can't make promises. And I have a full-time job. This is your project. You'll have to do the legwork."

But I can tell from the tone of his voice, he likes this idea. When Dad is in favor of something, he's like my two-year-old brother. He won't give up until he gets his way.

"The high school band could play at the game half. If Mr. Kelly can put an article in the News, we can advertise the game there. We'll invite all these famous people."

"I know," Beverly says. "Let's have a fundraiser and charge a small fee to come to the game, then we will donate the money to Martin Luther King, Jr. He can use the money for equal rights."

"Or we can donate the money to the National Organization for Women, the group my grandma belongs to. They want women to have equal rights, and this is what we're working for, Crackers' right to play with the boys."

"This is a great idea, girls!" Dad says. "I'll head into school tomorrow and check the gym calendar. By Monday morning we should have a date and time, then coordinate the other details."

"We will put a list together of who we want to invite. And Beverly and I have signatures for our petition. We can have a separate petition at the game for adults to sign."

"You have a plan," Dad says with pride.

We stand up and link our arms, jumping for joy.

CHAPTER TWENTY-NINE

CRACKERS JUMPS ON THE BED UNTIL MY BODY IS airborne. We are laughing so loud, Mom knocks on the door and asks us to pipe down. In between shushing each other, we can't stop giggling. Crackers falls to her knees and keeps bouncing like a Mexican jumping bean. Tears tickle as they roll into my ears.

"Wait!" she says. "I almost forgot." She hops off the bed and unzips her duffle. "Where the heck is it? I didn't forget, did I? I know I stuck it in the bag!"

I have visions of a magician's hat, Crackers pulling scarves, rabbits, and swords from her overnight bag. She tosses something over my face, and I scramble to pull off the soft fabric. A sock comes at me next, then she says, "Bingo!"

"What? What did you bring?"

Knowing Crackers, she's brought a midnight snack. Beef jerky or maybe a sandwich.

She climbs back into bed and hands me an awkward contraption. My fingers travel over a curved metal cage with a plastic base. As I look further, I examine an electrical cord. What the heck?

"Where's an outlet?" She's heaving blankets over my head, smacking me in the face with pillows.

"Why do you need an outlet?"

"Duh! Because I have to plug this in!"

"Are you going to tell me what's going on, or keep me in the dark?"

"You're funny, Hattie. Keep you in the dark. Hilarious. It's a work light. One my dad uses on cars, so it's super bright. I'm going to plug it in. Your room is pitch dark. I'll hold the light under my face, and you can try to see me. You practiced with a flashlight in the closet, but you didn't try to see anything but the light."

Sometimes I don't give Crackers enough credit.

"But what if I can't see you?"

"You'll be able to see me. I'm sparkly and shiny!"

We fall into a giggle fit again and can't stop.

"Shh. If my mom comes back, we're going to be in so much trouble."

"Trouble, bubble. Stop being such a worrywart."

"You'd never say that if you saw my mom mad. She grows horns, I swear."

Crackers snorts. "People are mad at me all the time. I'm a pro at winning them over. Plus, your mom really likes me."

"Because you're Eddie Haskell from Leave It to Beaver. 'You look lovely today, Mrs. Cleaver. You make the best pie, Mrs. Percha.' I'd feel so fake if I said those things."

"The pie was delicious!"

"True."

"I plugged in the light. Now, we go under the covers, sitting up, and I'll turn the switch. Don't cheat and tell me you see me if you don't just because you hear me flick the knob."

"I'm not a cheater."

We scoot down in bed and make a tent with the covers. Crackers' knees are touching mine. The blankets form a perfect cone around us. We go quiet, and after a minute Crackers turns on the light. At least I think she does. She's playing with the switch and making noise. Wait. She's being Crackers. She's trying to trick me.

"Tell me when you see the light."

We could be in a movie with a line like that. "I see the light! I see the light!" I start snickering at the thought and Crackers slaps my knee.

"Stop it!" she says. "Be serious."

The light goes on. I know because the beam is shining in the dark. A circle of light.

I'm dead quiet, narrowing my left eye, and raising my hand to touch her face. The difference is, rather than groping in the dark like usual, I see an outline. A round face. Crackers' face. I can sort of tell where her nose juts out just by looking— the shadows of her nose and cheeks, eyes and chin take shape. I swallow hard.

"Hattie, are you okay? What's wrong?"

I blink once. Then again. "I can see your face. Not clearly, but the silhouette. It sort of reminds me of these cutout things Mom had done of each of us kids when we went to Greenfield Village. This lady in an old-fashioned dress had me pose in a chair and she picked up scissors and cut this perfect shape of my face in about two minutes."

"Let me turn to the side. Look again."

"Your nose and chin stick out." I reach out and touch her nose. "This is your nose, right?"

Crackers drops the light in her lap and throws her arms around me. "You can see, Hattie! You can see!"

"How did you come up with this idea?"

"I was lying in bed thinking about how you saw the flashlight in the closet and I remembered Dad's work light. He goes under cars where there isn't much light and then when he turns this light on, he can see little parts he needs to work on. I figured the more wattage a light has, the better for someone who can't see so well. And this metal cage protects your fingers from burning because the bulb gets so hot, so it must be one of the strongest lights there is."

"You're really smart."

"I know, Hattie. I'm brilliant."

"Let's try other stuff. I'll shine the light and you tell me what you see. Practice makes perfect you know."

I see the palm of her hand and fingers extending out. "This is your thumb." I touch her thumb. "Over here, this is your pinky."

When she shifts on the bed and holds up her foot, I see her toes wiggle. "Feet are gross. I hate feet."

"Stay on track, Hattie. This isn't the time."

I fall into laughter again. She sounds like my mom. Funny. One day at my house and Mom is already rubbing off on her.

"Wait till Beverly finds out. She's going to go crazy!"

"She'll do a cartwheel. When I can see again, you have to teach me how to do one."

"It's happening, Hattie. You're not going to be blind forever."

"Let's see what else I can see."

CHAPTER THIRTY

Mom invites Crackers to attend Mass with us Sunday morning.

"I haven't been to church in a long time, Mrs. Percha. And I didn't bring a dress with me."

"You could borrow a dress from Hattie," Mom suggests, but I can tell from Crackers' voice she'd rather not come. She'd have to sit still and be quiet. A stretch for her.

"Dad's expecting me home. He should be here anytime to pick me up."

"The invitation is open."

"Maybe next time," Crackers says as she fills her mouth with half a pancake.

I already have my dress on and the boys are done eating, so Dad is shuffling them through dressing and putting on their church shoes.

The doorbell rings a few minutes later and Crackers hops up from the table. "Phew! That was a close one."

We snicker and head to the door. I open it for Mr. Mc-Cracken and he steps inside. "Thanks for having Crackers over, Hattie."

"We had fun."

I'm already sleepy since we were up practically the entire night, but Crackers is her usual self, springing up and down like a coil wound too tight. "I had so much fun, Dad, and I'll tell you a secret about Hattie when we get in the car."

She spins toward me. "I can tell him, can't I?"

"Sure, but not until you get in the car. I want to tell Mom and Dad too, but I'm waiting until after church."

Mom comes into the hall to say goodbye and Crackers blasts by me. "I have to give you a hug, Mom, and remind you to have me again soon. I'm happy to help with the dishes or whatever you need."

I can't help but shake my head. Crackers surprises me all the time.

After Mass, Dad drops off the family and asks if I want to join him at his school. Our little secret, setting up this basketball game.

He drives down the street and I can't wait any longer.

"Crackers brought a cool light from her dad's toolbox and we tried an experiment last night."

"What?" Dad asks as he turns down the radio.

My heart might explode. "I can see things when there's a bright light. Not the same as I used to, but outlines and shapes. My eyes are healing! I'll be back to normal soon."

"Was this Crackers' idea?"

"She's so smart! I love how she was thinking of me. Maybe if we have brighter lights at home and school, I'll be able to see even more."

"Winter's so gloomy. I bet once spring is here and we have more sunshine, you'll be able to see even more."

"I wanted to tell you and Mom at the same time, but I couldn't wait!"

Dad pats my knee. "Perfectly understandable."

He pulls into the lot and parks and we trudge through the snow into the hollow high school halls to check the gym calendar.

"Will you look at that!" Dad says.

"What?"

"We can sign out the gym next Sunday morning. We will have to rearrange our church schedule, but I say the sooner we hold this game, the better. You think the Dream Girls can pull this off in a week?"

"Of course we can! We're the Dream Girls!"

"I'll make some calls. Get the word out. I'm sure Grandma and Mom will do what they can too."

"Officer Nichols knows famous people, I bet, and Mr. Mc-Cracken can invite all his friends from work. We might have standing room only!"

"You may not sleep much this week."

"I'll sleep later!"

Dad chuckles softly before we walk the lonely halls to the band room. "I have access to a mimeograph machine for flyers. You call Crackers and Beverly from my office and make sure the dates work. Assign them different tasks. Didn't you girls have a list started yesterday?"

"Beverly wrote everything down. She's the club secretary."

"Call her first and have her divvy up the jobs."

Thirty minutes later, our plan is in motion. Beverly and Crackers are pulling together players for the game, Dad found an official who will referee, Grandma is handling the phone and written invitations—they have to be done pronto, since time is short.

As Dad says, "The wheels are in motion."

Monday morning at the start of school, the Dream Girls stand inside the entrance doors handing out flyers to each student. Maxine collects signatures for the petition and asks kids to bring their parents to Sunday's game and sign the adults' petition when they come. The air is buzzing with excitement.

Even Mrs. Foster stands nearby, encouraging kids to share the game information with their parents and their parents' friends.

Crackers makes kids promise they will come and support her. She has a crowd around her, both boys and girls, pinky swearing. "If you believe I can play basketball as well as anyone in our school, come to Cody High School on Sunday at 9 AM to support me."

Grandma wanted us to ask for donations from the attendees and then have the money go to the National Organization for Women as Beverly suggested, but Dad thinks people will be less likely to attend the game if we make the event controversial.

"The game will turn into an altogether different affair than intended if we get off track," he said. I trust him on this, even though Grandma will be disappointed.

From the way the halls are bustling this morning, our real goal, gathering support for Crackers, has a great start.

Mrs. Simmons meets me outside the classroom. "You and your friends are quite the rebels."

I'm not sure if she means this in a good way or a bad way.

I wish I could see her face. "We believe in Crackers. She's an amazing athlete."

"You're right," she says, and places her hand on my shoulder. I guess she's proud of us after all.

"You're very brave. Beverly and Crackers too. Just be prepared to be disappointed. Things don't always go as you'd expect."

I'm not sure what she means by this either, and my stomach goes queasy. "Do you think we're doing something wrong?"

"I don't know about wrong, Hattie. I worry this game you're planning could backfire on you though."

On my tenth birthday, the riots started, so I had to cancel the party. Does she think more riots will start?

Crackers elbows her way between us and squeezes my elbow. "Can you dig it? Everyone is coming! This is so groovy."

We wander into class to find out how many signatures we have collected. "Where's Beverly? Does she have all the papers?"

"I think so," Crackers says. "She and Maxine had their heads together when I came upstairs."

"Maxine," I say under my breath. "I never would have thought..."

I can hardly concentrate through the morning's lessons and when I make my way to Miss Tyler's room, I'm lost in thought and smack into a trashcan. Another bruise on my knee, no doubt. Pretty soon I'm going to resemble a bunch of grapes.

Miss Tyler stands at her desk when I enter the room. I decipher her outline with the sun pouring through the window behind her.

"Miss Tyler, I see you!"

"Good morning, Hattie."

I tell her all about the light game Crackers and I played over the weekend, how I'm beginning to see outlines and shapes.

"Wonderful news!"

"Do I still have to study Braille?"

"Knowing more than one language is always helpful. And you can't see well enough to read yet. Let's continue with your studies, but I'm also going to put some light on the subject. I have a light box in the closet. Let's see what you can do!"

Miss Tyler ransacks her closet, pulling out all kinds of stuff, and says, "Here it is!"

"What will we do?"

"When you and Crackers were doing your experiment with light the other night, you discovered how added illumination helps you see. With this contraption, I can place objects on top of the light. You may be able to see them and pick them up, or see enough to identify them. We'll try a few exercises and see how you do."

Butterflies flutter in my stomach. I want to see so badly, my heart hurts. I only have six days until Crackers' game, and the thought of not being able to watch her show off for the crowd makes my stomach sink.

Miss Tyler places a few items on the light box, turns out the overhead light and asks me if I can identify the objects. I can't, but I can tell if something is round, long, oblong, or pointy. I could tell the pencil from its shape, but the other things, no such luck.

She tries something cool next. She places a glass of water on the light box, then adds something to the liquid. I take a guess, "Did you color the water? I can't tell if I'm imagining or not, but it seems kind of red."

"Well, done." Miss Tyler rests a hand on my shoulder. "We will include some light therapy during our time together."

"I want to be able to see again." Tears flood my eyes, even though I'm at school, trying to be brave and unafraid.

"Your feelings are completely normal. Now that you can see shapes and differentiate things, you're more anxious than ever for your vision to come back. Try to be patient."

My voice crumbles. "Everyone always tells me to be patient...I never am. I...can't be. Ever...even before my eyes stopped working."

Miss Tyler wraps her arm around my shoulder. "I know, honey. I know."

I sob on her shoulder, soaking her blouse, and she pats my back, soothing away my sadness. After a long minute, I'm able to stop crying and blow my nose. "I'm sorry for crying. I try not to be a baby, but with Crackers' game coming up and all, I...I have to be able to see by Sunday."

"If I had a magic wand, I'd wave it over your head and say some special words to restore your sight."

"I need a miracle."

CHAPTER THIRTY-ONE

POSTERS LINE THE HALLWAYS AND KIDS CHATTER HOW the game is just two days away. Coach Mulder lets Crackers practice with the team all week, and her opposition looks steep. Several of Crary's players are on her team for the Sunday game, but the kids recruited from other schools are seasoned sixth graders. Chris Thomas, the boy I met at Rouge Park, plays for the other team, and Matt says he's the best defensive player on St. Mary's squad.

I haven't seen or heard from Chris since the day at the park, so now I have another reason to be nervous. I can't root for him if I'm cheering for Crackers.

Beverly says, "Chris must be nice or he wouldn't have agreed to play Sunday. He'll understand why you're cheering for Crackers."

My brain plays tug of war with spinning thoughts. What if no one comes to the game? All the kids will come, I'm sure, but what if none of the big wigs come? Will Chris talk to me? I tried counting sheep the other night when my head was so full of worries I couldn't shut off my brain to sleep, but I'm the same way during the day, and there aren't enough sheep in the world to distract me.

We didn't have a ton of time to alert the Pistons and the newspaper and TV stations—they might not be able to come. Then, all our efforts will be in vain. We have to make a difference. Beverly reads the paper every night. No articles about our game.

Beverly says, "We can't see the future. We don't have a lucky charm. There's no sure thing in life—except chores and homework." I'm sure she's right, but I'm awful tired of hearing the words over and over again. They're like a scratched record, repeating and repeating until my head is about to explode. I wish she'd just say, "Don't worry your pretty little head, Hattie. Everyone will come and support Crackers. The world will change overnight. She'll be allowed to play on the boys' team. Life will be perfect. Your vision will come back. All racism, prejudice and inequality will disappear."

At least Tommy's campaign to keep kids away from the game is sort of fizzling. His dream-killer attitude has about two fans. At least I'm hoping that's still the case and he hasn't organized some undercover boycott. Too many kids love Crackers to miss her show off her talent. Plus, Sunday morning means church and this is a great reason to skip, or at least go early and have something fun to look forward to on an otherwise boring day.

"Hattie?"

I hear my name from some far away place, like an echo in a cave, then again.

"Hattie?"

I tip up my head. "Yes?"

"I asked if you would like to tell us about the three types of rocks."

"Oh, sorry." Distractions and school don't mix. "Sedimentary, igneous, and metamorphic."

"Yes, those are the types, but can you tell us something about each."

Rocks. Rocks. Rocks. "Sedimentary are formed from particles of sand, shells, pebbles, and other little bits of material... called..."

I have to pay better attention.

Maxine whispers from behind me, "Sediment."

"Right," I mutter back. "Sediment."

"Igneous rocks form from the cooling of magma or lava," Crackers adds.

"Thank you, Ms. McCracken," Mrs. Simmons says, "but I was asking Hattie."

"I just wanted you to know I'm paying attention," Crackers says.

The class begins to titter.

"And remind you about the game Sunday. You're coming aren't you, Mrs. Simmons? I'll arrive at Cody plenty early. If you want, I can reserve you a front row seat. You're the guest of honor, really, because you're my teacher."

I know the face Mrs. Simmons makes. Her tight lips tip to the right, fold back into her cheek with a slight air of disgust, but secretly, she's fond of Crackers, and doesn't mind the interruptions. Not anymore.

"Thank you for the invitation, Ann. I will be attending."

"Should I reserve a seat for Mr. Simmons as well?"

Now the class falls out with laughter. Mrs. Simmons never

talks about Mr. Simmons. It's like he's made up. An imaginary husband. We've decided he's an apparition, like a ghost, since there isn't a picture of him anywhere. And when we ask her things like "Did you have a nice weekend?" she acts all private, like what she does on her own time is some kind of covert operation—teacher during the week, foreign spy on the weekend.

After we stop howling at Crackers' outrageousness, we wait in collective silence for Mrs. Simmons' answer.

"Yes, please."

Another reason to be excited for Sunday. We will finally meet Mr. Simmons. Woo-hoo!

Crackers walks me home from school. I've loaded my school bag with encyclopedias, even though the librarian doesn't usually let us check them out. But the Chaney branch is over a mile walk, and the school librarian took pity on me. Being blind has a few advantages.

Crackers is hardly a book person, she'd rather dribble a ball, but she agreed to read to me, and that's a victory all on it's own. The fact that Mom offered to let her stay for dinner might have added more than a little incentive.

"Mom, I'm home!" she yells as we dart through the back door.

"Hi, honey," Mom says, buying into Crackers' pseudo adoption. I think Mom secretly wanted another girl, but would never admit it. She wouldn't want my brothers to think she doesn't love them. Not that Crackers is a typical daughter or anything, but Mom can hardly resist Crackers loving her. No one can.

"Look, Hattie, Mom's set out cookies and milk for us." I smell the melting chocolate and feel the warmth of the oven as I step into the kitchen. Mom loves baking, but she sure seems to bake more often now that Crackers is her second girl.

We each sit down and devour a bunch, even though Mom warns, "Don't spoil your dinner."

Crackers snorts. "Can't say I've ever spoilt my dinner." She says spoilt like she just invented the word and she's looking for a reaction from Mom.

Mom doesn't say a word. I guess because Crackers has a point. She's never turned down food.

After our snack, I make her read to me. We haven't been able to find out a ton about women's basketball, and what we did is a bit disappointing, but that won't stop us. We'll never give up.

"The first women's game was played at Smith College. They didn't allow men to attend."

"I think that's an all-girl school," I interject. "Like Mercy High School."

Crackers sits so close to me I feel her shrug. "Not that I care if boys are allowed into a game, but if I can play as well as any guy, then they'll have to be allowed in.

"Looks like a lady named Senda Berenson was a lot like me. Ahead of her time."

Crackers stops reading, and goes stone quiet for what seems like forever.

"Well? What else did you find out?"

"Hold on. She's amazing, Hattie. She was sick when she was a kid and only when she was older did she get better. She did gymnastics exercises to improve her health, then became a teacher at Smith College. She tried to teach gymnastics, but no one was into that in the dark ages, so she tried basketball. Can you imagine? That's so cool!"

I wrap my hands around her arm and squeeze. "Tell me

more."

"She pushed for gym classes for everyone. Like she was one of the first people to realize the importance of exercise. Isn't it amazing that as a woman she could do that, way back then?"

"When?"

"1893. That was an eternity ago."

"Holy moly."

"Listen to this. The players wore bloomers."

The thought of women playing basketball in bloomers makes me giggle.

"This is a little disappointing," Crackers adds. "She wasn't into competition, just playing for fun."

"So, she's a tad different from you." Crackers, the most competitive person on the planet, can't relate. I get that.

"She demanded that players get good grades, or they wouldn't be allowed to play."

"That rule still exists today." I know this from Dad's teaching. He has to report grades for the athletes. If they fail a test during the week, they can't play in the next game.

"I wish you could see this, Hattie. It's a photograph of a ladies' team. The girls all have 1902 on their uniforms, maybe for the year, and they even have the date stenciled on a basketball. Their uniforms look a lot like nuns' habits, but they all have their hair pulled back and some of them are sitting in wicker baskets. I think they used those for their goals. I love this."

"I can see it in my mind. I bet they are really happy."

"You're right. They're all grinning."

"Here's another picture. Senda wrote a book too, 'Official Basketball Guide for Women,' published in 1915. She made up rules and everything. The players had to wear their hair in braids or tied in ribbons so they kept a tidy appearance."

I hold my belly I'm laughing so hard. I can't imagine Crackers wearing ribbons in her hair. Especially not while she's playing basketball.

"I can't wait until I can see well enough to read again. Senda sounds like our kind of girl."

"All in due time, Hattie. All in due time."

CHAPTER THIRTY-TWO

I START POPPING CORN AS SOON AS I WAKE UP. I WANT IT TO be fresh, and I have to get it all popped, buttered and loaded into bags before church. Mom finds me wagging the pan over the flame.

"Hattie," she says, like she's surprised, or shocked, or maybe even a little mad that I started without her. Not because she's so anxious to do the job, but because she's afraid I might burn the house down. I hold the lid on tight and shimmy the pot back and forth. When the lid pushes off the top and I don't hear much in the way of popping, I know it's done.

I finish making four batches, load the buttered and salted popcorn into brown paper lunch bags and staple them shut. Matt says, "What are you, blind? You're spilling popcorn all over."

"Darn it. Help me, would you?"

Matt leans in front of me to clean up the floor, grumbling under his breath.

Mom and Matt agreed to run the concession stand for us before the game. I'm so nervous, I'm glad to do a job that has me hopping around like a freaked out frog. I can't stand still.

"Do you think we'll have a big crowd?"

Mom hems and haws. "It's hard to say, but from what you've told me, you've sold lots of tickets."

"We need the right people there."

"I know what you mean, but if things don't go as you hope..."

"You mean nobody famous comes and takes a stand?"

Mom unfolds bags and snaps them open, adding more popcorn to each. "Honey, change takes time."

"I don't get it. Why does change take so long? And why aren't people smarter? You know Colleen Baldo's parents put their house up for sale, just because of the riots. If people move out of Detroit, how will that help solve the problem? Isn't that like running away when your city needs you the most?"

"Yes and no. The world isn't black and white like you'd like to believe, Hattie. It has many shades of gray. I imagine the Baldos are trying to keep their family safe. They think Detroit is a dangerous place now."

"But if everyone leaves the city, no one will be here to put things back together. Things will be even worse!"

Matt struts in front of me and offers his two cents. "Yeah, Mom, haven't you figured out Hattie is the next Rosa Parks?"

"I have to get ready for Mass," Mom says, as she races out of the kitchen.

I turn toward Matt. "Not Rosa Parks."

"Who then? Eleanor Roosevelt?"

"I'm Hattie Percha, and yes, someday I hope to be as famous as those brave women, but it's not about being famous."

"You're trouble. I have to admit, I'm a handful, but so are you, Hattie, just a different kind, and maybe worse." Matt whistles, and I imagine him cocking his head as he follows up with a low chuckle. He jabs me with an elbow. "You let Mom make all the popcorn, didn't you?"

"No, as a matter of fact. I did it myself."

"Well, aren't you the star blind girl."

"You're being a snot, and I'm tired of it."

"Just being myself, Hattie, don't you understand me?"

"Because I can't see, I'd think you'd be more sympathetic. But no. You tease me. You're evil."

"You have all these highfalutin ideas about changing the world, you're gonna have to toughen up. Just trying to help out."

"You're an idiot."

"I'm on your side, Hattie. We're more alike than you think. I agree with you about civil rights, and about Crackers playing basketball with the guys. She's a great player. She deserves a spot on the team."

I plop down in a chair and hold my head in my hands. Seems like everyone is changing on me all at once.

"I don't know about you, but moving beyond the lines is harder than I thought."

"You're pretty funny, Hattie."

I tramp over to the stove, grab the popcorn pot and plunge it into soapy dishwater. We have to leave soon, and I can't be late. "How do you figure?"

"You're one of the toughest girls I know, yet you don't believe it. You might want to start believing in yourself more."

CHAPTER THIRTY-THREE

IT SEEMS RIDICULOUS TO GO TO CHURCH TODAY. WHO CAN concentrate on God when the big game is right after church? Plus, wearing a dress to a basketball game seems… wrong. Just wrong. Then again, Chris will be there. Maybe he'll see me after the game. I twirl a lock of hair around my finger.

I pray through the entire Mass. *God, please let a reporter come and write an article about the game. Let one of the Pistons come and tell the schools to let Crackers play on the boys' team. Put Crackers on TV. Make the world right.*

I don't feel an ounce of divine intervention. No miracle juice is flowing through my veins. God isn't talking to me. Neither are Jesus or Mary. Some days are like that. Matt whispers as if he can see inside my brain, "If you ask God for things for yourself, they won't come true."

"God isn't a genie in a bottle," I hiss at Matt, even though I know I'm praying to God like he's a magician—Houdini or Harry Blackstone.

Mom shushes us.

By the recessional hymn, I'm fighting off a sinking in my chest. My heart is in my stomach, shooting straight for my toes. We cram into the car, which smells of popped corn, nauseating if you ask me. There are a hundred little bags loaded in the way back, so we're like a jar of those little sausages, all squished inside, and Dad drives down Grand River chastising us for complaining, picks up Grandma, and then turns on Joy Road.

When we arrive at Cody High School, Dad parks by the band room door and ushers us inside. Everyone has a box of popcorn bags to carry and we march to the gym where we set up tables. We arrange the snacks and Mom puts out a cash box and a sign. POPCORN 5¢.

We hurry inside and stake out some front row seats, Dad, me, Matt, Rob, Larry and Johnny. Matt is supposed to be helping Mom and Grandma, but as usual, begs his way out of the job.

I can't stand the anticipation. Where is everyone?

"Dad, I'm going to stand by the door. I should be there to welcome people, in case they don't know where to go."

"Go ahead, Hattie. The custodian should have the door unlocked by now, but you can check. Sitting here will make you crazy."

Dad understands. He doesn't try to change me.

I tap down the hall with my cane, the route to the entrance carved in my memory. As I crack open the front door, an arctic breeze rushes through and I shiver. I wait for what seems like an eternity, then finally, car doors' slam and voices echo in the parking lot.

Crackers' voice rings out, "Hattie-go-Battie, how the heck are you?"

I wrap my arms around her and squeeze. "You're here! Are you nervous?"

"Nerves are for people who have something to be afraid of! Can you dig it?"

I nod. "I can dig it!"

We tramp down the hall to the locker room. Crackers removes her long pants and tugs on shorts and a jersey. Her team is wearing blue—the opponents are wearing red. It's odd, her being the only player in the girl's locker room. She doesn't even have the chance to talk to her teammates.

Beverly joins us a minute later. "You look great, Crackers! Like a real basketball player."

"Let's get out there and see who's here!"

We dash into the gym and I can tell from all the noise, a decent crowd is gathering. "I saved us front row seats," I tell Beverly, tapping my cane to find the spot where I laid coats across the bleachers. "Is your family here?"

"They're sitting right behind your dad and brothers. Let's grab our places."

We gather Crackers in a Dream Girls' hug, wish her luck, not that she needs any, and leave her on the court with her teammates, ready to warm up. Balls begin bouncing and the air sizzles with excitement.

On our way to our seats, someone grips my arm. It's Tommy, the kid who complained to his dad about not making the team. He started this, yet he has the nerve to say, "Girls…you should be home playing with dolls—not allowed on the basketball court."

I'm so tempted to spout something nasty, but Beverly tugs at my other arm. "Time for us to practice cheers, Hattie. See you later, Tommy."

He heads to the other side of the gym, since he's decided to root for the enemy.

"Ignore him," Beverly says. I'm sure her back is straight as a post, her shoulders set like a soldier's and her head postured forward. Her "Beverly" pose. When she's put up her guard, no one can possibly penetrate her shield.

"Sometimes I get so mad, I feel like I'm going to boil over."

"I know." Beverly leads me to my seat and instructs me to sit. I follow orders and grasp her hand so she'll stay right beside me. "You have to tell me everything that's happening. If you see any celebrities from the TV stations, or any of the Pistons, let me know."

"I hate to break it to you, but I don't know any of the Pistons. I have no idea what they look like."

"No problem. Here's a gigantic clue. They'll be tall, way over six feet, and they'll be black, like you. Most of them anyway. Happy Hairston is like Paul Bunyan. And there's Walt Bellamy. Dad told me he's 6'11", so you'll be able to spot him from a mile away."

"Are there any white players?"

I giggle. "Of course! Don't be silly."

"Honest, Hattie, I'm not into sports."

"If I didn't have all these brothers, I wouldn't be."

"I have brothers too, but I'd rather bake cookies or read than watch a stupid game."

I whisper in her ear, "Never let Crackers hear you say that. You'll be in for a heap of hurt."

"Oh boy," Beverly says as she leans across me.

"What is it?"

"Mrs. Simmons just walked in. With Mr. Simmons. He's a hunk."

"A hunk?"

Beverly lets a "whew" sneak out from between her lips. "Hold on, I need to swallow."

True, Beverly's boy crazy, but I'm shocked to hear her mooning over a grown man. I listen to the girls around me. They're doing the same thing.

"He looks like Paul Newman."

"Can you believe those eyes?"

"No wonder she doesn't bring him around. She's afraid someone will steal him."

I lean over and say to Beverly, "Oh, now I get it. He's a dreamboat. I wouldn't have guessed that."

"Never make assumptions, Hattie. They'll get you in trouble every time."

Beverly stands and shouts at Mrs. Simmons, pointing out seats a few feet away from us.

We grasp hands as the buzzer sounds, announcing the beginning of the game. No one makes any announcements, like why we're all here today, and I wish I'd written a speech explaining things. Then again, maybe it's better this way—just pretend this is a normal game among normal kids, no mention of a girl taking on all the best boys in town.

"What's happening?" I ask.

There's shouting and Beverly screams over the hullaballoo, "Crackers has the ball. She's dribbling down the court. She passed it to another player. They're going in for a shot. Oh no!"

"What's going on?" I forgot to ask God to make me see today. Big mistake.

"Some boy knocked Crackers down."

"Is she okay? Is she getting up?"

"She's up! Dusting herself off and patting another boy on

the butt. You know how they do that? Why do they do that?"

I start to giggle, picturing Crackers slapping some random boy on the butt. This is ammunition. I tuck it in the back of my brain. I might need to get Crackers back for something someday.

"Wait, Crackers just got the ball. She's headed for the basket. She shoots. She scores!"

Beverly is up out of her seat, cheering, "Go Crackers!"

I join her, the pain of not being able to see Crackers' every move chewing at my heart.

I sidle over next to Dad. "Is anybody here?"

"Lots of people, honey. We have a great crowd. About seventy-five or eighty folks. Lots of adults, but more kids."

"What about Bill Bonds, or one of the Pistons?"

Dad's so into the game, it's as if he forgotten why we're doing this. "I don't know. Watch the game. Crackers is doing great!"

"You have to tell me each move like they do on TV. You have to be a sportscaster for me."

"Red has the ball. The tallest guy, a forward, is setting up a play."

"Who is he?"

"I think he goes to St. Mary's. He looks like a kid Matt knows."

Flutters flip my stomach upside down. "Is it Chris? Chris Thomas?"

"Hold on, I have to watch this play." Dad flies up out of his seat.

If I stand up, I won't know any more than I do sitting down. I wish I'd stayed outside with Mom selling popcorn. Then I could talk to people who come through the door. See if someone comes to scout Crackers. Instead, all I can do is have a pity party. Everyone can see the game. Everyone but me.

I stand, clasp my cane and sneak out the side door of the gym. I find the bathroom three doors down on the right. They leave the door open so teachers can catch kids smoking. Dad says students try to sneak cigarettes, even ninth graders. I slink into the bathroom and find a corner. I slither down the wall, slap my hands over my face and have a good cry. Gut-wrenching sobs echo in the concrete space, but I know no one will hear me—there's so much noise coming from the gym.

Though Mom warned me I'd face disappointment, I'd lied to myself—told myself everything would go my way. *By Sunday, a news reporter will be in touch with me, or Beverly, or Crackers. By Sunday, Grandma will get some famous lady who is changing the state of equality for women in the United States to come and make a ground-breaking speech telling the schools to let Crackers play on the boys' team. By Sunday, I'll be able to see.*

I cry and cry until my tears run dry, and stop to catch my breath. *Pity parties are for babies,* I tell myself. I pull up to the edge of the sink and splash my face with cold water. Crackers will kill me if I miss the entire game.

I make my way back to the hall, the cheers echoing from the gym erasing my sadness and pulling me down the hall. Before I know it, I'm on my face, my legs and arms splayed on the floor like a bear rug. I reach around but can't find my cane.

"Can I help?"

"I'm okay," I answer, hurrying to smooth my skirt and stand up.

The voice comes again. "Are you sure you're all right, Miss?"

"Yes, thank you," I answer.

"I hear a game going on. Shall I escort you into the gym?"

The words sound from far over my head. It's like God finally showed up, because the voice is deep and resonant, like I imagine God's would be.

He hands me my cane, then offers me his arm, as if he knows exactly how to lead a blind girl down the hall. We walk together in silence, but there is still a conversation going on between us.

CHAPTER THIRTY-FOUR

"LET'S SIT RIGHT HERE," HE SAYS, GUIDING ME TO A bleacher near the goal.

I straighten my skirt as I sit next to him. "What's the score?"

"Blue – 22, Red – 11. Do you have a friend on one of the teams?"

"Her name is Crackers. She's playing the game today to prove she's as good as any of the boys."

"On the blue team? Blonde curly hair? Lanky arms and a shot that doesn't miss?"

My face brightens. "Yep! That's her!"

The crowd woops and hollers, roars filling the air.

"She scored!" says the man beside me.

"Could you please keep me posted? Let me know every time she scores?"

"I'd be happy to, Miss." Every now and then, his rich voice informs me, "Two more points…Nothing but net. She swished the free throw…Wow, that girl can pass…"

I'm as proud as I've ever been. Crackers plays her best without a single hesitation. She's simply being herself.

By the end of the third quarter, the score is Blue – 30, Red – 22. "Red is catching up. That's not good."

"The point is to play as hard as you can, no matter who your opponent is. You never worry about the score, but do your very best. How did you hurt your eyes, young lady? Did you have an accident or have you always been blind?" the man asks.

"I was injured in a fall. The doctor thinks my vision might come back, and lately I can see light and dark and some shapes, so I think it won't be long now."

"You know, when I was a boy, I nailed two sticks together to make myself a hobbyhorse, but fell when I was running to show my mom. I accidentally poked my eye with a rusty nail."

"That had to hurt. Is your eye okay?"

"We were poor, so my parents couldn't afford an operation. My eye healed on its own. I've never been able to see the same since, but I wasn't about to let that stop me."

"I'm the same way. I want to see again, and I try to do everything sighted people do. Today though, I miss being able to see. I want so badly to see my friend play her favorite game and prove that's she's as worthy as any boy to be on the team. But mostly, I try to figure out ways to deal with bum eyes. I have to work at not letting being blind get me down."

"We all have those days," he says, a gentle tone riding in his voice. "No harm in having a moment or two when you wish things were different, just don't let those dips become habits. The more positive you are, the more good things will come your way. My eyes are fuzzy…will be my whole life, but I'm used to them. If you're a barrier buster, you won't let a single obstacle stop you."

A barrier buster. He's like a Dream Girl. Maybe I should invite him to be a part of our club. "Did God send you? We went to church this morning and I prayed and prayed. I felt like God wasn't listening, but you seem like an answer to my prayers."

He chuckles like spirit-lifting music. "I'm just a friend. What's your name, by the way? I'm Dave."

"I'm Hattie. It's nice to meet you. Thanks for sitting with me."

"My pleasure, young lady."

The buzzer sounds and the final quarter begins.

Sitting next to Dave is the best thing to happen to me in a long time. He's expert at telling me what's happening, like a real sportscaster. "She just landed a great jump shot. The girl springs like a gazelle. Another two points for your friend, Hattie. She's one of the best players I've ever seen!"

"Do you think she's good for a girl?"

"She's just plain good. By anybody's standards."

"You sound like someone who knows."

Another low chuckle. "I know a little about basketball."

"If you'd like, I can introduce you to Crackers after the game. She's one of my best friends, and she'd love to hear from someone who knows the sport."

"I'll be privileged to meet your friend," Dave says.

At the end of the game, the buzzer sounds. Blue wins! At least Crackers will be happy about winning, even if we didn't have the newspaper reporters or TV personalities or famous people. Mom warned me. She was right.

You can't change the world every day.

CHAPTER THIRTY-FIVE

THERE'S PLENTY OF COMMOTION AFTER THE GAME.

"Can you please tell me what's going on?"

"Everyone is celebrating. Looks like your friend was the high scorer this game. Her teammates are lifting her onto their shoulders. She's feeling the rush of the game, waving her hands over her head."

I laugh until my cheeks hurt. "That's Crackers. She's amazing!"

"How 'bout you introduce me to her?"

"Sure. Can you steer me?"

"Here," he offers, "take my arm."

We move over to where the players are standing. There's a sudden hush over the crowd, then people start murmuring.

"Hey..."

"That's...uh..."

"Why, it's Dave Bing!"

"Dave Bing from the Pistons."

"Beverly?" I call out. "Is that you?"

"Hattie, where have you been?"

"Sitting at the end of the row. I had to go to the bathroom, and then…"

"You mean you were sitting with Dave Bing this whole time?"

"No, I was sitting with a man, but his name was…Holy Moly! I was sitting with Dave Bing? The Piston? How did you know it was him?"

"You were the one who told me how to spot a Piston, silly. You said 'tall and black.' I don't know if it's Dave Bing for sure. There could be another Dave on the team, I guess. But everyone is saying it's him. It must be!"

When we spin around to investigate, Beverly gives me the report. "He's talking to Crackers, Hattie. This will be the best day of her life!"

"The Dream Girls have done it again!"

"Hattie, the Dream Girls is the best idea you've ever had.

"Dream Girls. It's the best name for our group, because all of our dreams come true!" Beverly stands back and rests her hands on my shoulders. "I know we gave you a hard time when you had the idea, but I sure am glad you made us do the club. Now, we're friends for life."

"Grandma thinks I can change the world. Mom and Dad agree, but they don't believe it as much as Grandma."

"We'll show them!"

By now, the entire crowd recognizes Dave Bing and kids and their parents line up for his autograph.

"He's still standing with Crackers," Beverly says. "Can you see the flash? Everyone's snapping photos. You'll love this, Hattie. Your mom just had a photo taken of her and Crackers."

"How do they look?"

"Your mom looks really proud. You know Crackers. She's pretty much always happy, but she's got her arms wrapped around your mom in a big hug. It's like a mother daughter photo. Aw, now she's back with Dave Bing. I don't think Crackers has blinked since he went over and shook her hand. There isn't much that shuts her up, but she's just staring at him now, her blue eyes twinkling, and a grin from ear to ear!"

"I can see her!"

"You can? You can see?"

"I mean I can picture her."

"Oh. Sorry." Beverly's voice drops, sympathetic and sad.

"Don't feel sorry for me. Ever. I've got this."

Beverly rubs my arm. "Let's go over and talk to them." She leads me over and Mr. Bing stops signing autographs for a minute.

"Ladies," he says. "I didn't mean to steal the limelight. Would you mind waiting for me a few minutes?"

"Not at all," I say, grasping Crackers arm. "We'll wait over by the bleachers."

Once we reach the front row, we take a seat and a woman joins us.

"Hello," she says. "My name is Marilyn Turner. I'm from Channel 2 News."

"Aren't you the weather lady?" Crackers asks, then leans toward me and whispers, "They sent her because this isn't a big story. If they were serious, they would have sent Bill Bonds from Channel 7."

I interrupt her. "Nice to meet you, Miss Turner. Thanks for coming today. Did you see the game?"

"Yes, I did, and I'd like to commend you on your amazing

performance today, Ann."

"You can call me Crackers. I never answer to Ann."

Mr. McCracken stands next to us. I smell his aftershave.

"That's my daughter," he says.

"You must be very proud," Marilyn adds. "Would it be all right if I interview her?"

"Be my guest."

"I've also been talking to some of the teachers from your school. I understand you girls have a club. The Dream Girls?"

"Yes," Beverly answers as she lays a hand on my shoulder. "Hattie's idea. Crackers and I are the other members and our mission is to do our part to make the world better. We want everyone to have the same opportunities, and help make dreams come true."

"We've already decided to go to the same college," Crackers pipes up.

"You're quite the triad, aren't you?"

My chest puffs out, and I imagine Crackers and Beverly standing as straight and tall as California redwoods reaching for the sun.

"Girls can do whatever boys can," Crackers says. "We just need the chance."

My mouth drops open. I had no idea Crackers would just spit it out, but I shouldn't be surprised. She's just being herself. Telling it like it is. My heart floods with pride.

"Why don't we get Mr. Bing and the girls together for a short news segment?" Marilyn Turner says.

Dad and Officer Nichols join us and give us permission to talk in front of the cameras.

"Your mom and grandma are watching, Hattie! They look so proud of you," Beverly whispers.

I peer over her shoulder, struggling to bring them into view. As hard as I try, I can't really see them, can only guess they are gathered close to us. There are so many people—I don't have a way to distinguish them from anyone else.

Dad leaves for a moment and returns with Dave Bing. I spot him, because his shape is the tallest and darkest under the gymnasium lights. The news reporter asks him a few questions, which he answers all at once.

"My friend Happy Hairston was invited to attend today's game but had a prior commitment. When he mentioned the circumstances, I thought, why not see for myself? I wanted to see this young lady, Crackers, and what she could do on the court. I must say I'm very impressed. I'm not about the news media, you know that, Marilyn, but I am a fan of young people who are interested in making the world a better place as these three young ladies are doing, and I'm always eager to witness new, raw talent."

"How do you feel about Dave Bing attending your game, Crackers?"

"Totally groovy. A guard with Mr. Bing's talent coming to watch little old me play basketball is far out. Maybe because he's here today, he'll find a way for me to play on a boys' team someday. That would be so cool."

Marilyn Turner interrupts. "Tell us about your club, Hattie."

I turn to Marilyn Turner's voice. "Like Beverly said, we started the Dream Girls a few months ago, but I didn't know we'd make a difference. That happened accidentally."

"Beverly, can you share your experience with the Dream Girls?"

"I'm the first black girl at Crary. Hattie and Crackers welcomed me to the school when other kids didn't like me. Hattie and Crackers didn't care. Now I have two of the best friends ever."

"We want the world to be a better place. Not everyone is convinced that we're right about being friends with people who are different from us, but Beverly, Crackers and I are determined to show them how it's done," I add.

Crackers elbows me and whispers, "Good one, Hattie."

"You're impressive young women. We hope to hear more from you in the future."

Miss Turner ends the interview and Dave Bing places his gigantic arms around our group.

"How would you girls like to come to a Pistons' game?"

"Yeah baby!" Crackers springs off the floor about a zillion feet into the air. Her cheer rings down from far above my head. She's back to her old self, which I find reassuring. If she acted like a grown up all the time, I wouldn't recognize her. Good thing about Crackers, she knows when to turn on the charm.

"Thank you, Mr. Bing," Beverly says, "but I'm not a huge sports fan. Could my dad come instead?"

"I'll give you tickets enough for each of your families. How about that?"

Crackers hits the ceiling again, whooping with joy.

"Thank you," I say. "My brothers will love watching you play! You're Matt and Rob's favorite Piston."

"I'll make sure to reserve courtside seats for all of you. And Hattie, the announcers will give you a play by play, so don't worry about not being able to see the game."

CHAPTER THIRTY-SIX

GRANDMA INVITES ALL THREE FAMILIES TO HER FLAT after the game. We squeeze into her front room and she serves coffee to the adults and sets out a plate of cookies in the kitchen for us kids. We follow the scent and eat until we're stuffed, gabbing about our front row seats at the upcoming Pistons' game.

Crackers leans over to Matt, "I'll make sure you and Beverly sit next to each other at the game."

Matt jabs me in the side with his elbow. "See, Hattie? Even Crackers thinks Beverly and I should date."

"You're too young. Mom and Dad already told you."

"What about you? I saw you talking to Chris on the way out of the high school." Matt's mocking me.

I blush, my cheeks growing hotter by the second. I didn't think anyone had noticed my quick chat with Chris.

"What did he say?" Beverly asks.

"He told me I looked nice, and congratulated me on having

Dave Bing come to the game. I told him I didn't do anything, but he didn't believe me. He thanked me because he got an autograph. Chris is good enough to play for the Pistons someday, isn't he?"

Matt guffaws. "Hattie's in love. She has stars in her eyes."

I slap his shoulder. "Knock it off. You're so obnoxious."

Grandma calls us into the front room to watch the 12 o'clock news, poised and ready. If we miss it now, we won't see it. Not like a national story they'd repeat on tonight's newscast. We sit two deep on the floor in front of the TV, shushing each other. My heart pounds so hard I worry it will dwarf the volume of the television. I grip Beverly's and Crackers' hands and squeeze them so tight, Beverly shouts, "Ouch! Ease up, Hattie."

Crackers giggles. "I'm a star!"

Mrs. Nichols shushes us and bounces baby Larry on her knee.

The news anchor announces the segment and the room goes silent. You can't even hear anyone breathing. I wait in the dark until Marilyn Turner asks Dave Bing the series of questions and he responds.

"What can you see? Can you see us? Can you see Crackers?"

No one answers me—they are all too busy watching. The movement of hands flashes in front of me. Fingers pointing at the television set, I guess. "There's Crackers!" Matt shouts. "I see Beberly," Ricky, Beverly's little brother says.

"Am I there too?" I ask.

Johnny shouts, "Hattie!" so I must be there.

We can hardly hear the reporter's comments over the commotion we make. Everyone inches closer to see the screen. When this happened at home before I lost my vision, no one could see and we ended up fighting. I don't hear arguing yet, but Beverly decrees, "Down in front. I can't see."

Crackers jumps up, leaping so hard the floor shakes beneath us. Funny how her dad doesn't stop her. My parents would cream me for acting so rambunctious.

"I'm a star! I'm a TV star!" she shouts. "If Senda could see me now."

An abrupt quiet settles over the room within seconds. "Interesting story, Marilyn," the news anchor says. "And now for the weather." Our story is finished.

We can't contain ourselves, and neither can Mr. McCracken. He's so proud.

"I know this is an unusual request," he starts, "but I'm wondering if you would consider letting Hattie and Beverly spend the night at our place. We haven't had an overnight at our place since...well...in a long time. I promise to make the girls go to sleep at a reasonable hour. Seems like they deserve some time together after all their hard work to make this day happen."

My parents would never ask a question like this out in the open in front of us kids, but then Crackers' dad isn't an ordinary dad, or she would be an ordinary kid. A hush fills the room for a full sixty seconds before Mrs. Nichols speaks up.

"How nice of you to offer, Fred. We don't allow Beverly to have sleepovers on school nights..."

"But maybe just this once," Officer Nichols interjects. Beverly and Crackers whoop for joy, and I stand in front of Mom and beg, "Can I? Can I, please?"

Mom sighs and her frustrated breath washes over my neck. I recognize that sigh. It's her giving-in breath.

The Dream Girls hold onto each other's shoulders and cheer louder than the entire crowd who attended the game earlier.

"We can drive by your houses and pick up your things," Mr. McCracken adds.

"Let's get this party started."

I know Mom wants to warn me to go to bed on time, but thankfully she doesn't embarrass me. My family just puts on their coats and hats and follows the Nichols out the door while Grandma packs us a box of cookies to snack on later. We have the entire afternoon and evening to ourselves. Maybe life could be better, but I can't imagine how.

Once we arrive at the McCracken's, Crackers leads us up to her room and we spread our sleeping bags out next to her bed. She pulls hers out from her closet and squeezes it in between ours.

We sit in a circle and talk about the game, the newscast, and how much we hope everyone watched us. The rest of the world fades away and we completely wrap up on our own little sleeping bag island.

Mr. McCracken delivers pizza and Coca Cola in bottles about dinnertime, I guess. We eat and talk and talk and eat, diving into Grandma's cookie stash and finally, after hours of conversation, snuggle down in our blankets.

Once Crackers turns out the light, I have a burning question that I finally work up the nerve to ask. "How did I look?"

"What do you mean, Hattie?" Beverly's voice turns serious, just as I would expect.

"Just wondering if you can tell I'm blind."

"You do a good job faking it, Hattie," Crackers whispers. "I don't think anyone can tell unless they notice your cane."

"Not like that's easy to hide."

"I wonder if anyone famous saw the broadcast. Do you think the newspaper will want to do a story about me?"

Crackers. She has a way of showing us what's really important.

CHAPTER THIRTY-SEVEN

I STIR ON THE FLOOR, REALIZING THE SUN SHINING THROUGH the window is what woke me. I alternate closing my left eye, and then my right. I can see shapes outside the window when my right eye is closed. Probably tree branches, because the shapes dip and turn and grow out of each other. "Hey, you guys. Wake up. My eyes are getting better."

I shake Crackers' shoulders and give Beverly a light kick with my toes. I run my fingers over Crackers face, then close my right eye and study her. "I think I can see your eyes."

I point my finger at the spot and she shrieks. "Hattie, that hurts! Knock it off."

"Wait, Crackers," Beverly says. "This is the best news. Hattie's getting better. Just like we've been praying. Try looking at me, Hattie."

I turn to face her and see the outline of her Afro. Her hair is sticking up like she put her finger in the electric socket and I can't stop laughing. "Your hair is crazy!" I touch a tuft here and a tuft there, all the while marveling at the sight.

"Far out!" Crackers says, and she boings Beverly's hair as she makes a popping noise.

"That's enough," Beverly announces and tramps out of the room and down the hall.

"You could be nicer," I advise Crackers.

"You could see better," she retorts.

We fall into a giggle fit until Mr. McCracken knocks on the door and reminds us to get ready for school.

Half block from school, Crackers begins muttering, "I wonder if they'll come."

"Who?" I ask as Beverly steers me around a fire hydrant.

"Be careful, Hattie," she says, "there's a dog pile in front of you."

Crackers stops to look. "Where?"

I veer to the left and get back on the sidewalk. "Will you just answer me? Who will come to school?"

"The Detroit News, or the Free Press."

"I wouldn't count on it."

"Now you sound like Mom. What a downer, Hattie."

A smile grows across my face. Crackers is part of my family now. Just what I always wanted.

We join our classmates before the bell. I write a story in my head. One where Crackers gets called to the office for an offer of a college scholarship, the first of its kind being offered to an elementary school student who has displayed talent worthy of such an award, then I hear the morning announcements. The usual warnings about ice on the playground and reminders to turn in overdue library books. On the tail end, right after Mrs. Fletcher clicks off the microphone, she comes back on.

"Ann McCracken, will you please report to the office?"

Jitters fill my stomach, and my brain starts to buzz. "This is it!" I whisper. "You're famous!"

Crackers stands and I see her hands shoot over her head. "It's okay, everyone. Don't worry. I'll never forget who was in my corner when this all started."

We fall out laughing, and Mrs. Simmons doesn't even try to shush us. "Miss McCracken can let us all know if she has any news when she returns to class."

Crackers bounces out of the room like a kangaroo, hopping and putting on a show. I can't see her perfectly, but I can see her jumping with both feet. It's all a blur, but knowing her like I do, I can imagine the look on her face.

Time drags for the next half hour. I can't see the clock, but we aren't being assigned homework yet, and Mrs. Simmons is still teaching us about why "it" is a bad word to use in our writing. "'It' stands for something. Increase your vocabulary. Use rich details and nouns to pull us into your stories."

Normally, I'd be right with her, thinking about new words I want to use in my writing, but Crackers has been gone so long, I'm starting to worry. Maybe she's in trouble of some kind. Maybe all our efforts on the game caused a problem and she's the one who's hearing first. Worrisome knots replace the jitters and I can hardly pay attention. I lean over to Beverly. "What do you think is wrong? Why has Crackers been gone so long?"

Beverly shushes me, but I know she's worried too, because there isn't a lot of fervor in her "shhh!"

My foot taps on the floor, waiting, waiting, waiting. Worrying, worrying, worrying.

I hear the click of the door knob, and notice the familiar footsteps as they trap through the classroom. Mrs. Simmons continues teaching, not stopping for a single beat. I can't stand waiting. Crackers doesn't make a sound once she reaches her seat. Nothing's right. Nothing's normal. I'm dying for information, but Beverly has already warned me to be quiet.

"Beverly," I whisper. "C'mon, you have to tell me something."

"I don't know, Hattie. I can't tell."

I start to ask her another question, but Mrs. Simmons interrupts. "Hattie, Beverly, we're still having English class, in case you haven't noticed. You can talk at recess."

Recess. Schmecess. That's at least an hour away. The suspense is killing me.

We finally finish two hours of boring work before Mrs. Simmons says, "Ok, class, let's take a break."

I'm up out of my seat clattering my cane against the desks and almost out the door before Mrs. Simmons calls out, "Hattie, come back to your seat. You'll be the last person out of class today."

Crackers shouts, "Yeah, Hattie, it's my job to get out of here first. Back to your seat, young lady."

The class titters and I crash into three kids on the way back to my desk, but I don't even care, I'm so focused on making it out of class and to the playground so I can find out what the heck is going on.

Maxine stays back and offers to help me down the stairs. "Thanks, Maxine, but I'm good today."

I race as fast as my tentative steps will carry me, and finally reach the playground. I call Beverly's name above the hoots and hollers of a hundred screeching 5th graders. "Where are you, Beverly?"

"Here," Beverly answers and grabs my arm.

"Where's Crackers?"

"Playing football as usual." The winds whips my hair across my face and Beverly tucks it back inside my hat.

"She must be in trouble, or she would have waited for us."

"Stop being such a worrywart. She'll tell us when she's ready."

My patience flew out the door as soon as I came outside. I can't stand waiting.

"Let's go by the fence and do handclaps."

Beverly leads me across the playground, past Crackers and the boys, and the swing set, monkey bars and slide, and we assume our usual spot at the edge of the yard. We start clapping our hands together and reciting one of our favorite rhymes, when Crackers darts in between us.

"Wanna play?" she asks.

"Play what?" I'm sure she doesn't mean football, unless she's entirely lost her mind.

"Bad thing, good thing," she says, a snide tone filling her words.

My face lights up. "You first."

"I want Bev Jo to go first," she says, placing her hand on my arm.

"Beverly?" I say.

"Bad thing that happened today was I forgot my English homework. Good thing, I wrote a few sentences out really quickly when Mrs. Simmons sat at her desk to write a note, so I didn't get in trouble."

I stand stone silent when Beverly finishes. I want to jump up and down and tell Crackers to fill us in right away, but knowing her, she'll make us wait, just to drag out the agony.

Beverly speaks up. "Crackers?" she says in a slow drawl, as if she's trying to pull words out of our friend.

"Bad thing first."

My heart clenches.

"I had to come to school today."

Beverly and I groan.

"Good thing. Coach Mulder received the tickets for the game. They're right here in my hot little hand." She pulls her hand from her pocket and waves them in front of us. We screech and jump up and down. This weekend. Sunday afternoon. Just a few days away.

CHAPTER THIRTY-EIGHT

S IF TIME WAS SUSPENDED, MINUTES REFUSED TO PASS
no matter how hard I tried to will the clock's hands
forward, but Sunday finally arrived. As an added
blessing, church went by in a blur, and before long the time
came to head to Cobo Hall for the game. Courtside seats, as
Dad calls them. For our entire family.

My brothers whoop in the halls, and Mom rushes around
barking out instructions, "Get your shoes on. Coats everyone.
Be sure you use the bathroom before you get in the car. Even if
you don't think you have to go. Try."

I'd give anything to ride with Crackers, but Mom says this
is a special day for her. Since she's the reason we have a fistful of
tickets for all of our families, she deserves this time alone with
her dad. We can sit together once we're at the game.

I hear packages crumple. Mom stuffs her purse with
snacks—"I refuse to pay a fortune for candy." Sometimes, she
cracks me up.

We finally pile in the car and make our way downtown. Even though I can't see well, I can make out outlines of the tall buildings, and there's an air about the city, the exhaust from the busses and smoke from the Ford factory. We're getting close.

Mom rattles on about how great the city looks, and how lucky we are to be Detroiters, in spite of the riots. She's being optimistic. Some parts of Detroit are still recovering and buildings haven't been rebuilt yet, but I'm with her. I love the Motor City. I'm proud to call myself a Detroiter.

Dad parks in the lot and we shove each other out of the car, Mom instructing the boys, "Hold my hand, Johnny. Matt, carry Larry for me, would you?"

I can't wait to get inside and see my friends. All I can think is *hurry up. Hurry up.*

Mom lines us up behind Dad as he talks to the usher in front of us. The usher says, "Follow me." We troop in behind him like baby ducks and follow him all the way down the steps of the arena to the very first row. Thankfully, I could hold onto the railing almost all the way down. Otherwise, I might have needed my cane, and I left it in the car. On purpose.

When we finally reach our seats I realize Dad is right. We are sitting courtside. For real. The players are warming up and I can feel the thump of the ball as they dribble, and the whoosh of heavy air as they pass.

I tug on Matt's arm. "Is Cracker's here? Help me find her."

Matt's nice, for once. "Come on," he says. "I'll take you over to her."

I hear her two seconds later, "Hattie, Hattie, almost blind as a Battie. Give me a hug, chickadee. This is the best day of my life."

My heart smiles as big as ever. I'm so happy for her.

We find Beverly and everyone makes room for us to sit together—me, Crackers, then Beverly. Having Crackers in the middle makes the most sense. She's the real guest of honor, not the two of us.

There's a ton of noise. An organ plays. Vendors shout, "Popcorn, get your popcorn!" and "Hot dogs, fresh and delicious!" Fans chatter and cheer. My brothers have pennants, which they are waving in our faces. I don't mind the feel of the felt on my face, but knowing the boys, they'll poke me in the eye with one of the sticks.

Crackers grabs one of the pennants and jumps onto the seat of her chair. I can picture her hopping around, and I hear her cheer, "Pistons, Pistons, Pistons."

A buzzer sounds and I hear a whistle shortly after the players run onto the court. The game begins.

I can't see much, but flashes of legs stream by me. The pounding footsteps, the smack of the ball against the court, the shouts of the players and fans echo through the air. This close, I can hear the players call to each other as they set up plays. The rush of excitement is enough, listening to Crackers hoot and holler and give me the blow by blow even though I hear the announcers, "Two for Bing…oh, dang, fouled again. You should see this, Hattie."

She's having a total blast. As she should.

Halftime comes soon enough, and the best part is the Pistons are ahead by eleven points over the Los Angeles Lakers. We're winning!

"Can you believe we're here?" Crackers still can't control her excitement.

Beverly says, "This is the very best day, Crackers. I'm so proud of you."

We hear an announcement above the crowd. "Would our special guest, Miss Ann McCracken, please join Detroit Pistons star, number twenty-one, Dave Bing, at center court? The announcer's voice reverberates and I hear the words repeat in my head. "Crackers, that's you! They want you!"

Before we know it a gentleman shows up to escort Crackers onto the court. She says, "Thanks," and races off in front of him. He's still standing in front of me, but she's long gone. Her voice trails off, "Mr. Bing. Mr. Bing. Here I am!"

Crackers. Never. Changes.

Beverly moves next to me and squeezes my hand. We don't need words right now—we know how we're feeling.

Dave Bing begins to speak. "We have an honored guest with us today. This young lady, a 5th grader at Crary Elementary School, invited her community to watch her play ball last weekend. She's one of the most talented new players I've ever seen. Mr. Zollner, the Piston's owner, heard me talking about this rising star during one of our practices last week, and when I mentioned having her as our guest today.

"Miss McCracken, we have a surprise for you today. You are hereby being awarded a scholarship to attend the Piston's Future Players' Basketball Camp. This is the first time a young lady will join the young men, but you certainly have displayed the ability and talent. Are you willing to accept the prize?"

All I hear is hooting and hollering, even though Crackers has to be a good fifty yards away from me. After her shouting dies down, I hear her, "Dream Girls? Did you hear that? Dad, did you hear? I'm playing basketball with the Pistons!"

She makes her way over to us and the Dream Girls wrap our arms around each other in a giant hug. Happy tears run down our faces as we stand cheek to cheek.

This isn't just a good day for the Dream Girls. This is the best day of our lives.

THE END

ACKNOWLEDGEMENTS

There are always an abundance of people to thank when one finishes a project of this magnitude. To my first reader, Don Whitsitt, for his endless support and five o'clock serving skills, thank you. To my children, Melissa, Noah, Katie and Jenna— thank you for encouraging me to keep on writing, I love you all. To Lori LaBoe, Ann McCracken, and Beverly Johnson, my undying appreciation for your inspiration. With heartfelt gratitude to beta readers Lori LaBoe, Don Whitsitt, Cynthia Nachtrieb, Katherine Pfieffer, and Angelle LeBlanc. To the countless teachers, students, and parents who express their delight about these books—your words matter. And to all those from the Southern California Writers' Conference—Jean Jenkins, Michael Steven Gregory and Jeremy Lee James—you continue to lift me up. Cheers!

ABOUT THE AUTHOR

Reading was Claudia's favorite subject in school, and writing came in a close second. Now she spends more time writing than reading, but doing what she loves has always been a priority.

Before Claudia retired from teaching, she promised her fifth-grade students that she would write them a novel. BETWEEN THE LINES was the result, BEYOND THE LINES, a sequel at their request. Sharing themes of friendship, tolerance, and respect, it is her hope that each and every reader will make a vow—to be kinder, to offer a helping hand, to lighten the load of their fellow man.

Claudia taught for thirty-seven years before trading her passion for teaching with her passion for writing. When she isn't writing or in the classroom sharing her love of reading and writing with students, she's enjoying the outdoors—walking, swimming, or traveling with her husband and friends. She lives in Michigan.

She loves to hear from readers, so please visit her website at www.claudiawhitsitt.com or find her on Facebook at Claudia Whitsitt, Author.

#friendshipiscolorblind